The Secret of the Sword

Christy Bower

*Austin,
Feed your
imagination
daily.
Christy*

Dragon Hollow Trilogy

The people and events depicted in this story are fictitious, which means I made them up. But don't tell them that. They are convinced they are real. But let me assure you that any resemblance to actual people and events is purely coincidental. However, if you find yourself being followed by a donkey, I am not responsible.

To Caleb and Nathan: Feed your imagination daily. You don't want to see what happens when it's hungry.

The Secret of the Sword
© 2013 by Christy Bower
www.DragonHollowBooks.com
ISBN-13: 978-1490457116
ISBN-10: 1490457119

Cover image © iStockphoto.com / papendesign

Chapter 1
Hide and Seek

The king shook his fist in the air. His face was almost purple with fury. "How dare you oppose your king!"

The entire council stood with their mouths open, uncertain how to calm their new monarch and make him listen to reason.

"King Burger, my lord, we do not oppose you. We only seek your best interests. Let's sit down to discuss how we can best handle this delicate situation."

"There is nothing to discuss. You will either do as I have ordered or you will be removed from the council."

"Sir, there is no point in having a council if you're not willing to listen to your advisors."

"You're right. This is a monarchy. I rule. I

don't need you. Guards!"

Several guards ran into the room from various directions.

"Kill them," shouted the king. "They are traitors!"

A great commotion broke out.

Peter, who had been hiding behind a curtain, whispered to Sebastian and Alexandra, "Let's go."

As they snuck out from behind the floor-length curtain near the hallway, a guard spotted them. "Intruders!"

"Catch them!" yelled the king.

A guard nearly grabbed them as they ran out the door, but he fell with a thud and blocked the way for the other guards, giving the kids a bit more time. Peter, Sebastian, and Alexandra ran down the hallway. They were headed for the spiral stairs but two guards were blocking their way.

Peter said, "Follow me." Then he dashed into a doorway on the left. They passed through a small meeting room for entertaining diplomats and entered a small kitchen for serving guests, which opened up into a full-sized kitchen. The kids knocked over some serving carts and a few large pots to slow down their pursuers.

The commotion drew the attention of other guards and, as the kids ran out the kitchen door, a guard stood ready. He grabbed Peter, but Peter stomped on his foot and got away. Then in a last attempt, the guard grabbed hold of Alexandra's skirt. She yelled and pulled away as hard as she could. Her dress tore and she was free.

They were in another hallway. Peter hesitated. Then he darted into a doorway. They ran through the library, with the sound of guards yelling and clamoring after them. Peter threw open the library doors onto the balcony. He looked down and said, "This will work." Then he jumped on the balcony rail and over the edge to a rooftop a short distance below. Sebastian helped Alexandra over the rail and then he jumped over, too.

Peter led the way across the roof to a trellis where they were able to climb down to the ground.

Just when they thought they were safe, a guard in the courtyard yelled, "There they are!"

Peter, Sebastian, and Alexandra took off running. Guards started appearing from every direction. The kids ran behind a building and some guards followed. Then they sprinted down a cobbled road, with guards in pursuit.

Peter suddenly got on his knees and crawled through a small hole in the hedge row. Alexandra followed him. By the time Sebastian started to crawl through, a guard grabbed his feet from behind. Sebastian kicked several times and finally planted a heel in the man's face. The guard let go and held his nose. "He broke my nose! That overgrown hedgehog broke my nose!"

On the other side of the hedge, there were more townspeople milling around. "Let's slow down. Try to blend in," suggested Peter.

They walked across a courtyard, surrounded by vendor carts and a few small shops. Guards began filtering into the courtyard, looking for them. For a minute, Alexandra thought the guards didn't recognize them, but then she heard one say, "Over there! It's them!"

"Let's go back to the castle," said Peter, beginning to run.

"What?" exclaimed Sebastian and Alexandra.

"It's the last thing they'll expect. We might be able to throw them off," said Peter, as they ran down an alley.

They followed the castle structure along a long stretch of wall. Peter said, "This is it." Then they walked through an arched entryway. "This is the servant's entrance," explained Peter. There was a quiet hum of activity as servants wandered back and forth completing their chores. Some carried clean linens for beds. Others carried baskets of fresh food. Others held pails and cleaning supplies.

"Look, Peter," said Alexandra, "some of the servants are about our age."

"Let's grab some linens or baskets and try to look busy," said Sebastian.

"Good idea, you two."

They went into a supply room. A steward there said, "Hey, what are you doing here?"

Peter stammered, "Oh, um, we want to know how to become servants here."

The steward replied, "In that case, my name is Myles. The new king does seem a lot more demanding than King Cole, so I think we could use a few more hands."

"New king?" asked Peter, hoping for more information than he had learned since his return to Mirabeau this morning.

"Yes. After the death of King Cole in the attack on Mirabeau, Ham Burger made himself king."

"How'd he do that?" asked Sebastian.

"There are several different rumors about that. Some say he paid the knights on the council to support him. Others say he threatened the knights. Most likely, both rumors are true. But it's not our place, as servants, to question the authority of the king. We are here to serve."

"What types of things do the kids do?" asked Alexandra.

"Young folks like you assist the servants in performing their tasks. You would be valets assigned to other servants. It's like being a servant to the servants until, with time and training, you become a servant."

"What do we do to become valets?" asked Peter.

"I'll arrange for you to meet King Burger. Come back, let's see now, I won't be able to speak to the king until tomorrow so I'll schedule your meeting for the following day. That will work. Come back day after tomorrow for your interview with the king. Everyone who works in the castle must first meet his approval. Since you're children and don't have any political loyalties, it probably won't be a problem."

"I hope you're right," said Sebastian, looking sideways at the other two.

"Thank you, sir. We'll see you then," said Peter.

Peter, Sebastian, and Alexandra discreetly left the castle to make sure they weren't being followed and they headed for the stable to find Donkey Oatie.

When they were in sight, they heard his loud "Hee haw." He ran to greet them. "I'm so glad to see you. I could tell something was amiss by all the guards patrolling the street."

"We're fine, but let's go in the stable to talk," advised Peter, looking around one last time.

The three kids flopped down on a pile of hay, which Donkey Oatie began to eat.

"When Lucas the Magician told me I was the son of King Cole and rightful heir to the throne, I guess I thought I'd walk home and everyone would crown me king. I never dreamed someone else would make himself king while we were off fighting the dragon. What a mess! What am I supposed to do? I'm just a kid. No one will believe I'm King Cole's son because I was raised by guardians. And after we snuck in the castle to check out the king, we found out he's extremely dangerous! It's not like I can walk in and announce that I'm the rightful king. He'd have me killed like he had his knights killed to silence their opposition on the council."

"And now that we're wanted as intruders, when the king sees us at the interview tomorrow, he may have our heads anyway," said Alexandra.

"Yes, but it's possible that the king himself did not see us well enough to identify us," said Peter. "Besides, working inside the castle will allow us to keep an eye on things and study the king so we know what's going on."

"Speaking of keeping an eye on things, have you checked on the eggs today?" asked Alexandra.

"Thanks for reminding me." Peter got up to retrieve his backpack, which contained his favorite book, *The Legend of Dragon*

Hollow, and two eggs laid by his former pet, Peeve. When they returned from The Magic Kingdom, Peter wrapped the eggs in cloth to protect them and keep them warm on the journey home.

He opened his backpack and said, "We're home, guys. Sort of." He reached in to grab the cloth and pulled his hand back as if he had been burned.

"What?" said Sebastian.

Peter sat down with the backpack and looked inside more intently. He carefully poked the cloth again. "Well, we have geckos."

Alexandra began clapping with glee. Sebastian moved in for a closer look as Peter carefully pulled out the cloth.

Two of the cutest geckos you'll ever see were cowering in the backpack, staring at the kids with huge round eyes that seemed too big for their bodies.

"Mama?" asked one gecko.

"Um, well, not exactly," said Peter.

The other gecko came to the mouth of the backpack and announced, "Happy birthday!"

"Happy birthday, indeed!" squealed Alexandra.

"Isn't this a pleasant surprise?" announced Sebastian.

The first gecko scampered over to Sebastian and stood on his hind feet. "Are you my mother?"

"No, but I knew your mother, Peeve," said Sebastian.

"How sweet!" said Alexandra.

The gecko scurried over to her. "Are you my mother?"

Alexandra giggled. "No. But we are all your friends and we will take good care of you as your mother, Peeve, would have wanted."

"What are you going to call them, Peter?" asked Sebastian.

Peter shrugged.

"Oh, let's name them," pleaded Alexandra.

"How about Fiery and Smoky?" suggested Sebastian.

"How about Blacky and Flame?" asked Alexandra.

"They're not even black. They're green," said Peter.

Donkey Oatie chimed in: "Okay, so if they're green, name them Booger and Snot."

Alexandra slapped Donkey Oatie on the hind quarter and he went "Hee haw." The kids giggled and laughed at his gross suggestion.

"Oh, how about Prince and Princess?" suggested Alexandra. The boys just stared at her. "Well, Peeve turned out to be a girl," she added.

Then all three kids started throwing out names rapidly.

"Jaggy?"

"Cinder?"

"Snout?"

"Cringe?"

"Mammoth?"

"Twang?"

"Quickee and Flash," said Alexandra.

They all looked at her for a moment.

"What? Geckos move fast."

"Blimpie and Slurpy," said Sebastian.

"I was thinking more like fierce dragon names like Devastator and Avenger. Or maybe Crusher and Smash."

"Oooh, those are good ones," admitted Alexandra.

Donkey Oatie chimed in again: "They'll grow up to be fire-breathing dragons so why not call them Burpy and Belch?" This comment earned another playful swat from Alexandra.

After some continued deliberation, Peter said, "I know what I'm going to name them."

"What?"

"You'll see."

Chapter 2
Chuck the Woodchuck

Peter went to the market to buy some food for the three of them. He heard, "There's one of them now!" He looked over his shoulder and saw two guards coming for him. He dropped his sack of vegetables and started to run, but he ran into someone and fell to the ground. Before he could get up, the guards grabbed him.

They hauled him off to the castle, where he was brought before King Burger. The king stared into the boy's eyes to intimidate him, but Peter said, "You're not going to get away with betraying the kingdom!"

The king yelled, "Traitor!" and drew his sword. The guards let go of Peter and backed away so Peter drew his sword, too.

Clang. Clang. Clang. Clash.

Peter's sword began to glow blue as he

met his opponent blow for blow.

Whoosh. Clash. Clang.

The two swordsmen circled each other, staring into each other's eyes.

Peter was soaked with sweat. The king was difficult to defeat. Peter was getting tired. His sword was too heavy and his more skilled opponent continued to meet him blow for blow.

Whoosh. Clang. Clang. Clang. Clash.

Then, in a moment of mental fatigue that broke Peter's concentration, the king flipped Peter's sword out of his hand. Peter turned to retrieve his sword and out of the corner of his eye, he saw his opponent's sword lunging toward him.

Peter woke up with a yell.

He was drenched in sweat. It was another nightmare. Ever since he had been injured in a swordfight with the evil sorcerer, Deofol, Peter had been having nightmares.

Wiping the sweat from his forehead, Peter got up to take a drink. It looked like Sebastian and Alexandra were still asleep on piles of hay. He looked out the stable window. The sky was always the deepest blue before sunrise.

Alexandra, who woke up when Peter yelled, was quietly watching Peter.

Peter pulled out his sword and began to study it. He rubbed the blade and could feel the inscription, but he could never make out the words for some reason. Sometimes, when he fought with it, the blade would glow blue and it seemed to reveal the words, but he couldn't take time to read them while he was fighting. It's not like he could interrupt a sword fight to say, "Excuse me while I pause to read my blade."

When Donkey Oatie saw Peter moving, he pranced over, "Good morning, Sir Peter."

"Good morning, Donkey Oatie. At least I think so."

"You think so?"

"Well, I had another nightmare last night."

"Oh, I see. You know, I have a very important question I've wanted to ask you. It's kind of personal, so I'm a little hesitant to ask, but I really want to know and you are the only knight I know so you are the only one qualified to answer."

"Donkey Oatie!"

"What?"

"Just ask."

Donkey Oatie looked at Peter with big, pleading eyes and asked, "Do knights wear knighties?"

Peter cocked his head, raised his eyebrows, and pushed his mouth to one side in a smirk that pretended to be annoyed but quickly broke into laughter. "Okay, you win. It's a good morning now."

When Sebastian saw Peter holding his

sword, he asked, "What's going on?"

Peter said, "Sebastian, will you fight me?"

"What?"

"You know, to see if the blade will glow blue this time so I can read the inscription."

"Oh, that again. We've done this before, but, sure, we can go a round or so. Right now?"

"Let's do it before adults start showing up around the stable yard."

"Okay, but let's make it quick. I'm hungry."

Both boys stood with swords in hand. Sebastian made the first move. They clashed blades again and again but Peter's blade didn't glow.

"I just don't understand it," said Peter once they stopped. "Why does it glow sometimes but not every time?"

"It's a magic sword," said Sebastian as he sheathed his own sword. "Magic is never predictable."

"I think it's like a mood indicator," said Alexandra. "You know, when you're intensely fighting, it glows."

"Perhaps," said Peter. "I wish I knew. I wish Lucas the Magician would have told me more. I wish he were here to explain things now. Everything seems so much more complicated now than when we were in The Magic Kingdom."

While the kids ate a quick breakfast of

bread and cheese, Donkey Oatie ate some oats. Peter, Sebastian, and Alexandra decided to go look around, although Peter warned, "Let's not wander too far off." They were ready to go and Peter said, "Are you ready, Donkey Oatie?"

"Miff a miffit," said Donkey Oatie with his mouth full.

The kids stood at the door, "Are you coming?"

"Yes!" He took another bite.

Then Peter hollered, "We're leaving!"

Donkey Oatie said, "Alright, alright, don't get your knightie in a tighty."

Next to the stable was the royal granary. On the side of the building was a small stream that turned a water wheel, which cranked a mechanism inside to grind the grain into flour.

Donkey Oatie trotted over with great interest. There, beside the water wheel, was a small creature tossing fire wood into a pile.

"What are you doing?" asked Donkey Oatie.

"Chucking wood."

"What for?" asked Donkey Oatie.

"Because that's what I do. I'm a woodchuck."

"A woodchuck?"

"Haven't you heard of a woodchuck before? You know, like in the verse?"

> How much wood
> would a woodchuck chuck
> if a woodchuck
> could chuck wood?

The kids laughed so he did it again.

> How much wood
> would a woodchuck chuck
> if a woodchuck
> could chuck wood?

Peter, Sebastian, and Alexandra thought this was very funny. "You're a delightful creature," said Alexandra. "What's your name?"

"Chuck."

"Of course," said Donkey Oatie, rolling his eyes. "Well, what's up, Chuck?"

"What do you mean? What is 'up-chuck'?" asked their small friend.

"Well, up-chuck is vomit, but I think Donkey Oatie is asking you 'what's up?' which is a way of asking 'how are you?'" explained Sebastian.

"Oh, I'm very fine, thank you for asking."

"Do it again, Chuck," pleaded Alexandra.

> How much wood
> would a woodchuck chuck
> if a woodchuck

could chuck wood?

"What's the answer?" asked Sebastian.

Chuck puffed out his chest proudly and said:

> He'd chuck all the wood
> that a woodchuck could
> if a woodchuck
> could chuck wood.

Chuck continued, "The verse presumes that I can't chuck wood at all, but clearly I can. As for the amount, I'm not really sure, but I can chuck this whole pile in ten minutes."

"Then what do you do with the wood?" asked Sebastian.

"I chuck it again, into another pile. I just keep chucking wood from one pile to another all day, every day."

"You must get tired of it," said Sebastian.

"Not really. It's what I do."

"I'm already tired of it," said Donkey Oatie, referring to the verse, not the work.

"Could you say it again? All of it?" asked Alexandra.

> How much wood
> would a woodchuck chuck
> if a woodchuck
> could chuck wood?

He'd chuck all the wood
that a woodchuck could
if a woodchuck
could chuck wood.

Alexandra clapped in delight. Donkey Oatie said, "He's not that impressive. I can do it, too!"

How much don
would a donkey key
if a donkey
could key don?
He'd key all the don
that a donkey could
if a donkey could key don.

Chuck's eyes got big as he looked at his long-eared competition.

The kids roared with laughter. Sebastian and Alexandra dropped to their knees and held their stomachs they were laughing so hard. Peter slapped Donkey Oatie on the hind quarters and said, "We'd better go, Donkey Oatie, before Chuck challenges you to chuck wood. Nice to meet you, Chuck." Peter winked at Chuck and they all went back to the stable.

When they went inside, they found the two geckos scurrying around on the walls and ceiling of the stable. Sebastian grabbed a shovel handle and started poking the ceiling to make them scurry around even more. Sebastian and Alexandra were giggling at the quick, erratic movements of the geckos.

Peter said, "I wouldn't do that, if I were you."

"I'm not going to hurt them."

"I was more concerned about them hurting you."

"A little gecko isn't going to hurt us."

One of the geckos began to glow red. "Peter, Look!" exclaimed Alexandra.

"Stop!" said Peter, just as Sebastian poked the ceiling one more time. The little gecko burst into flames, dropped off the ceiling and landed in a pile of hay. The dry hay began to catch on fire. Peter grabbed a horse blanket and threw it on the fire to smother it so the flames would go out.

The little gecko crawled out of the hay and looked up at Peter.

"It's okay, little buddy, you're okay." Peter picked him up and put him in his pocket.

"What was that?" asked Sebastian.

"Grudge."

"What?"

"His name is Grudge."

"And what about that red-hot flaming thing?" asked Sebastian.

"When Grudge feels threatened, he turns red and bursts into flames."

"So you knew about this before?"

"Yesterday, when I reached in my backpack to check on the eggs, I knew they had hatched because I felt movement. But as I grabbed one of them, I pulled my hand back suddenly because I got burned. I left him in there until he came out on his own."

"Grudge. Why Grudge?" asked Alexandra.

"Don't hold Grudge."

They all laughed.

"And what did you name the other one?" asked Sebastian.

"Hunch. I've got a Hunch."

They all laughed.

Chapter 3
Oh, Brother

Donkey Oatie wandered outside again so Peter, Sebastian, and Alexandra followed him. They played a spontaneous game of tag in the alley until they found themselves up by the old mill.

"What are you kids doing?" asked a man.

"Oh, hello. We were just playing tag," said Sebastian.

The sign above the mill said, "Swill Brothers Mill." Alexandra asked, "Are you Mr. Swill?"

The man chuckled. "Yes, I am one of the Swill brothers. My name is Phil."

"Phil Swill?" asked Alexandra.

"Yes, ma'am. And here come my brothers." Four others approached them and Phil introduced them. "This is Will, Bill, Gil, and Jill."

"Jill? I thought you were the Swill Brothers," said Sebastian.

Phil explained, "Jill is our sister but she has been part of the Swill Brothers for so long I don't think she knows she's a girl."

The kids looked at each other. Peter said, "My name is Peter and this is Alexandra and Sebastian."

Phil said, "Would you kids like to join us for lunch? We're going to put some fish with dill on the grill here at the mill."

"Oh, that sounds lovely," said Alexandra.

Phil asked, "What kind of fish are we having today, Bill?"

"Today's fish is krill. Will, did you kill the krill to put on the grill?" asked Bill.

"Yes, Bill."

"Jill, did you remember to pay the bill for the krill?" asked Gil.

"Yes, Gil, I signed it with the quill and now it's by the till," said Jill.

Peter, Sebastian, and Alexandra looked at each other, puzzled by these odd folks, who were dressed in no-frill twill.

Bill brought out his special dill sauce, but he tripped as he was carrying it. Phil said, "Careful there, Bill. Did you spill any dill?"

"Just a li'l. In fact, it was almost nil."

"Oh, Gil, did you remember to take your pill?" asked Will.

"No, but it's on the window sill by the till," said Gil.

"If I had the will, I'd walk up the hill to pick some fresh dill," said Phil, "but we'll use the Swill dill from the mill."

"Wait until you hear Will sing with a trill while he cooks on the grill," said Gil. "Sometimes his singing is shrill, but it's a thrill. I've heard him sing a thousand times, but I like it still."

"While we're waiting for lunch, would you kids like to see my skill with a drill?" asked Jill Swill.

"Sure, why not?" said Sebastian.

After the drill demonstration and a hearty meal of krill with dill cooked by Gil on the grill—and yes, indeed, he sang with a trill—Bill asked, "Did you get your fill of krill off the grill?"

Peter, Sebastian, and Alexandra assured the Swill Brothers that they had eaten more than enough dill-flavored krill. Then they thanked Phil Swill, Will Swill, Bill Swill, Gil Swill, and Jill Swill.

As they walked back to the barn, Donkey Oatie shook his head and said, "Oh, brother."

"What?" asked Peter.

"Was it just me or was there something kind of strange and annoying about them?"

The kids smiled at each other. Alexandra said, "What are you referring to?"

"You know, the way they played with words but it seemed like they didn't realize they were playing with words."

"Does that bother you?"

"Well, yes. It's kind of annoying," said Donkey Oatie.

"And you would never do that would you, Donkey Oatie?" asked Alexandra.

"Of course not. I don't invent ways to annoy people with words."

"Uh-huh," said Alexandra and she and the boys started snickering.

"What?" asked Donkey Oatie.

"Oh, nothing," said Sebastian.

Chapter 4
Little Orphan Army

A young boy was in the back of the stable cleaning out stalls when they returned.

Donkey Oatie pranced around and nudged Peter with his nose. "I've got someone for you to meet." Then he pranced to the back of the stable and said, "Peter, Sebastian, Alexandra, I'd like you to meet Pip."

The boy, about their age, said, "I see you slept here last night. Donkey Oatie tells me you're planning to stay here in the stable for a few nights."

"We won't be a problem for you. Please don't kick us out. We have nowhere to go," said Sebastian.

"Yes, I know. But I have a better place for you to stay. Lots of children lost their parents in the attack on Mirabeau, so an old lady started an orphanage. I don't want you to have great expectations," said Pip, "but it might be better than sleeping in a stable."

Peter turned to Sebastian and Alexandra. "Come to think of it, we might be better off if we blended in with other children."

"Good point," agreed Sebastian.

"I can take you there now, if you like," said Pip.

"That would be nice," said Alexandra. They gathered up their bedrolls and belongings and followed Pip.

As they approached the orphanage, they noticed it was a large building. But it had been damaged by the attack on Mirabeau so a large chunk of the upper right corner was missing. This made it sort of L-shaped. The remaining vertical section had a large crack coming down from the top, but the rubble was being held together with rope that gave the appearance of boot laces.

As they were all discussing the appearance of the orphanage, Pip explained: "Yes, it does look like a shoe or boot. The old woman who runs the orphanage has never turned away a child. But, honestly, I don't know how she does it. She has so many children she doesn't know what to do."

Donkey Oatie ran in front of the kids and stopped in their way. "Wait! Stop! You can't go there. I've heard of this woman. This is a bad idea—a very bad idea."

"What are you carrying on about, Donkey Oatie?" asked Alexandra.

"I've heard warnings. There's a song to warn children about her." He looked around nervously and whispered:

There was an old woman
who lived in a shoe.
She had so many children,
she didn't know what to do;
She gave them some broth
without any bread;
Then whipped them all soundly,
and sent them to bed.

"That's just a child's rhyme," said Sebastian. "There's nothing real about it. And it's just an odd coincidence that the old building looks like a shoe. Don't worry. It'll be fine."

"No, really. I have a bad feeling about this. I don't want you to get hurt," pleaded Donkey Oatie.

"Donkey Oatie, we can take care of ourselves," said Peter, drawing his sword. Sebastian followed his lead and drew his sword, too.

"Oh, yeah. Right. But, still, I'm warning you: this is going to be trouble."

The kids continued down the road but

they looked back to find Donkey Oatie sitting in the road still.

"Aren't you coming?" asked Sebastian.

"I think I'll go back to the stable where there's plenty of hay to eat," said Donkey Oatie.

"Suit yourself. That's probably a good idea. We'll see you tomorrow," said Peter.

"I hope I see you at all," said Donkey Oatie grimly hanging his head.

"We'll be fine," said Alexandra as they continued toward the orphanage.

"Oh, fine, I'm coming, too. All for one, and one for all," said Donkey Oatie. "Whatever happens to you, will happen to me, too." He trotted along to catch up to the kids. Alexandra rubbed his ears while they walked.

Dozens of kids were coming and going, climbing all over the rubble, or playing in the dirt. Some kids were stacking castle debris like building blocks. The older boys were making two forts out of rubble. Four boys were pretending to sword fight with sticks.

"A few months ago we were fighting with sticks, Sebastian," observed Peter.

"Yeah, and now we have real swords," said Sebastian. "We don't have to pretend to fight dragons or evil sorcerers anymore. We've done it."

Then a woman, with gray hair and eyes

that twinkled, approached them. "Hello. My name is Mamme. Welcome to the biggest family you could ever wish for."

"Your name is Mommy?" asked Alexandra.

"Mamme. It does sound similar, doesn't it?" said the woman with a smile.

"Do you have room for three more?" asked Sebastian.

"Room? I never have room, but that's never stopped me in the past."

Donkey Oatie chimed in. "It's like my mother used to say: do the best you can with what you have and you will have more than enough."

"I might have a way to help you with your overcrowded orphanage," suggested Peter.

The woman looked at him and raised her eyebrows, waiting to hear what he might suggest that she hadn't already considered.

Peter continued: "The new king is expanding the number of servants in the castle by bringing in children to serve as valets, or servants in training. They will be assigned to an adult servant. This sort of apprenticeship is valuable training. It would be a great opportunity for your older children here."

The woman brushed a wisp of hair out of her eyes and said, "That sounds like a rare opportunity."

"Yes, ma'am. And we have an interview

already scheduled for tomorrow morning, if the others would like to join us."

The woman took a few steps to the center of the yard, where she pulled a rope to ring a bell.

Sebastian elbowed Peter, "Are you sure about this? If we show up for our interview with the king surrounded by dozens of other kids, who knows what will happen?"

"What better way to blend in? We're already marked as intruders, but chances are no one will be able to pick us out of a large group of children."

"Brilliant," said Sebastian. "How do you come up with these things?"

Peter shrugged his shoulders.

When they heard the bell, children of all ages stopped what they were doing and gathered to Mamme.

"Children, we have some guests who would like to talk to you about a job training opportunity." She nodded to Peter.

Peter cleared his throat and spoke loud and clear to the large group assembled before him. For a brief moment he wondered if this is what it would be like to be king. Then he began to address the crowd.

"Hello, my name is Peter and this is Sebastian and Alexandra. King Burger is expanding the number of servants in the castle by bringing in young people to serve as valets. If you are interested in being a servant in training, you will be assigned to an adult servant who will guide your apprenticeship. It's a great opportunity to learn new skills and gain experience. It's also a way to become independent because you will live in the servant's quarters at the castle. Anyone who is ten years or older can go with us to the castle tomorrow for an interview with the king. If you are interested, stand by this tree so we can see how many will be going."

Kids began shuffling around and soon it was clear: they would have a very large group to take to the castle.

"Thank you. That will be all. We'll gather here after breakfast tomorrow."

"Mamme," said Sebastian, "I think we're about to help with your overcrowding problem.

Afterwards, a girl came up to Peter, Sebastian, and Alexandra. "Please, may I come, too? I'm eight years old, but I can work. The rest of us want to come, too."

Behind her, other children were watching and waiting from a distance.

"Why are you so eager to become servants and do the work of grownups?" asked Alexandra.

Looking around nervously, the girl whispered: "Mamme doesn't feed us that well. Maybe it's all she has, but all we get is broth for dinner."

Donkey Oatie cleared his throat and began to hum the woman-in-the-shoe verse.

Alexandra looked at Peter and Sebastian. The boys had their eyebrows raised because of what Donkey Oatie had said about this rhyme.

"Yes, of course. Anyone may come, regardless of age, but I can't guarantee that all of you will become valets in the king's castle," said Alexandra.

"Oh, thank you. All we ask for is a chance. Thank you. Thank you. Thank you," she said to each of them.

"What do you make of that?" asked Sebastian.

"I'm not sure," said Peter.

"You *know* what I make of it. That was no children's verse, it was a prophecy," said Donkey Oatie, nodding his head up and down for emphasis.

After an evening meal of vegetable broth, Mamme began to scold children for unfinished chores. Then she walked around the broken down house, ranting about this and that. Alexandra noticed that the smaller children hid in their beds long before bed time.

"We've got to get them out of here," said Alexandra. "All of them."

"I imagine they will all try to come with us," said Peter.

Alexandra counted as she climbed the ladder. She was in the fourteenth bunk bed. She was excited about sleeping so high up. Sebastian was in the one above her and Peter was in the one above him. They marveled at how Mamme had created a dormitory by stacking up the beds as high as the three-story structure would allow.

"Peter," whispered Sebastian.

"Yes."

"What is your plan? Or do you have one?"

"I've been thinking about that. I need to get assigned to a position that will put me as close to the king as possible so I can keep up with what is going on."

"Do you think that's wise? After all, you are a wanted man now. And the king is clearly dangerous. If you did anything to displease him, it would be the end for you."

"I know, I know. But there is a crisis brewing and I need to be ready for whatever happens."

Chapter 5
March on the Castle

Peter assembled his army of children and they walked a short distance to the servant's entrance at the castle. Donkey Oatie met them on the way. Peter motioned to the orphans, saying, "Wait here for my signal."

Peter, Sebastian, and Alexandra went into the storage room. Myles looked up from his work and smiled. "Welcome back. To be honest, I wasn't sure you'd come."

"You said you needed help so we came and we brought other recruits for you." Then Peter let out a long, shrill whistle.

Several dozen kids, of various ages, came around the corner, into view. Myles stepped out of the storage room for a better look. He stood in astonished silence for a moment. A low rumble erupted into a full laugh. He slapped his leg and laughed even harder.

The crowd of children looked at each other.

Myles stood up and regained his composure. "Well, the king will get everything he asked for and more. I have arranged for an audience with the king for the new recruits, so let's go—all of us!"

The steward led the crowd of children across the courtyard like an unruly army. Donkey Oatie followed along. He didn't want to miss a chance to tour the king's castle. They went through a series of passageways, up some stairs, down a hallway, and into a large banquet hall. "Don't wander off. I'll go get the king." Myles disappeared through a doorway.

The children whispered and looked around. This was a new experience for nearly all of them. Peter had been raised in the servant's wing of the castle, so he had explored the castle a great deal, without permission, as a young boy. But most of them had never stepped foot in the castle.

The king entered the room and stopped abruptly. "What's the meaning of this?"

"My lord, you asked for servants—young, un-political valets to be trained to serve you in all respects. So I have recruited a large number of orphans who will gladly serve you for food and a bed."

"Hmm. I see. I did ask for more servants

and I need some fresh blood that has no loyalties to old King Cole. We're leaving the past behind us. Young servants are good. We can train them to think the way we want, um, er, I mean train them to do things properly."

Myles said, "Of course we will train them properly, sir. Would you like to interview them?"

King Burger paced back and forth a minute, looking at the faces in the room. "What's the donkey doing in here?"

"I came to apply for the position of minstrel," said Donkey Oatie. The kids in the room laughed. "I can sing, and dance, too. I prepared an audition. Check this out." With that, Donkey Oatie cleared his throat and burst into song:

> I'm a honkey tonk donkey.
> Honky, honky, honky, honky.
> And I . . .

"Enough!" yelled King Burger.

"But it gets better. Give me a chance."

The kids were roaring with laughter because Donkey Oatie had been dancing to his lively tune—crossing one leg over the other as he side-stepped and kicking up his back feet for show. It was a sight to behold, and one which Peter, Sebastian, and Alexandra had seen before.

"Get him out of here!"

"Aww. I think you should keep him," said a young voice in the crowd.

A guard escorted Donkey Oatie out of the room. When the kids settled down, King Burger asked: "Have any of you been inside the castle before?" Four hands went up. Peter was the tallest so the king called on him first. "For what reason were you in the castle? Hmm. You seem familiar. Have we met before?"

Peter shifted his weight from one foot to the other and back again. "We have never met."

"Still, there's something familiar about you. At any rate, why were you in the castle before?"

"I lived in the servant's quarters."

"You were a servant before?"

"Not exactly. My . . . guardian . . . was the chief horse master in charge of managing the stables."

"I see. So you have some experience with horses?"

"Yes, sir. I grew up in the stables."

The children in the room laughed.

"Then I assign you to work in the stables. Report there after you are cleared by the physician."

King Burger questioned another boy, who claimed to have visited the castle for the king's annual festival. "So you liked King

Cole, did you?"

"I don't know, sir. I just liked the music and entertainment of the festival. It was a big production and a lot of fun. I look forward to the event every year."

"You'll do."

Then the king turned his attention to Sebastian and Alexandra. "And for what purpose have you been in the castle?"

"I came to the servant's quarters to visit a friend," said Sebastian.

"I, likewise, came to visit a friend," said Alexandra with her voice wavering.

"Fine. Since you two boys might know your way around a bit more than the others, I'll assign you to be my personal couriers, carrying messages to summon my servants and advisors as I have need. The girl can work in the royal kitchen. The rest of you appear satisfactory. If the physician says you don't have any diseases, you will be assigned to housekeeping, grounds keeping, or kitchen staff. You are dismissed."

With that, King Burger pivoted on one foot and marched out the door with an air of formality.

The children were escorted to another room where they waited to see the doctor. A man with funny looking spectacles came out to greet the children. "I am Doctor Zeus."

"Doctor who?" asked someone.

"No, Doctor Who only works on the weekends. I am Doctor Zeus. I will see each of you one by one, starting with the youngest, so please be patient. Thank you."

Peter, Sebastian, and Alexandra whispered among themselves.

Peter said, "I can't believe I got stuck way out in the stables. I wanted to be close to the king so I could keep track of what's going on. You two are right where I wanted to be."

"Well, I'm terrified of the prospect of working directly for the king. I'll be worried that I'm one mistake away from being dead," said Alexandra.

"Don't worry, Pete. We'll have access to important information and we can keep you informed," said Sebastian.

"How?" questioned Peter.

"I don't know. Let's think about that. I don't know how often we'll see each other. Maybe in the servant's quarters at night?"

"I have an idea!" said Alexandra, a little too excited.

"Shh."

She whispered, "We have two geckos that could carry our urgent messages back and forth among the three of us."

"That's brilliant, Alex. Why didn't I think of that?" said Peter.

Chapter 6
Secrets and Spies

Peter spent the day cleaning out hundreds of horse stalls. It was a familiar task that brought back memories of his childhood. *That's odd*, he thought, *I'm thinking of childhood as something long ago but adults still see me as a kid.*

He didn't mind working at the stable. It felt good to do some physical labor. And the solitude gave him time to think.

Everything seemed so strange and unexpected. He was the rightful king, but no one knew it. But it didn't seem right—or possible—to fight for his position. And yet this king was clearly a tyrant who needed to be stopped.

On the other hand, Peter didn't know how to stop him. More importantly, he didn't know if he even knew how to be king, if that ever really happened. *Life was so much simpler as a child,* he thought. *There I go again with the once-upon-a-childhood thoughts, as if my childhood were a fairy tale of the distant past.*

Odibrand, the stable manager, approached. "You've done a very thorough job, Peter. I'm impressed."

"Thank you, sir."

"I spent the day taking an inventory of how many horses we have. I itemized this list by chargers or war horses, then riding horses, cart horses, and packhorses. The king had a particular interest in the number of war horses available. We have 480 warhorses ready for battle, plus a few I'm trying to bring back to health, but they aren't included in these totals. As you probably know, we used to have about twice as many before the attack on Mirabeau."

"Yes, sir."

"Well, the king requested these numbers by the end of the day. Would you deliver this inventory list to the king—and deliver it personally? Then you can go home for the night."

"Yes, sir. As you wish. Thank you."

Alexandra entered the kitchen, but saw no one. "Hello?" She walked slowly into the room. "Hello?"

"Hello, young lady," said a chubby little

man with cheeks as red and as round as cherries.

"I'm a new valet assigned to the royal kitchen. Am I in the right place?"

"You certainly are. And what is your name, little missy?"

"Oh, I beg your pardon. Today is my first day and I'm very nervous. My name is Alexandra."

"Well, Miss Alexandra, I am the head chef, Oven."

"Your name is Oven? Like a kitchen oven? And you're a cook?"

"Oven is a Swedish name. And I prefer to think of myself as a chef rather than a cook."

"Well, I'm pleased to meet you, Oven, the Swedish chef."

"The pleasure is mine. The kitchen will be much merrier with a pretty young lady like you working here."

"You're too kind."

"Come. I'd like you to meet my bakers." She followed him into an adjoining kitchen, where a lady with gray hair and a plump man in a white baker's hat were up to their elbows in flour.

Oven said, "Alexandra, I'd like you to meet my cake baker, Elizabeth Crocker."

"You may call me Betty."

"And this is my pastry chef, Bill Spury."

"It's a pleasure to meet you all," said

Alexandra, feeling a bit shy.

In the throne room, the king instructed Sebastian, "Inform the kitchen chef that I will have a guest for dinner, so plan dinner for two in my private dining room. Then find the custodian, Mister Clean, and ask him to freshen up my private dining room for tonight's guest. Then go find Ludwig, the musician, and tell him the king requests music for a special dinner guest tonight."

"Yes, sir. With haste."

On his way out the door, Sebastian wasn't looking where he was going and he bumped into someone. He was startled a moment and looked up to see Peter standing in the hallway. "Peter? What are you doing here?"

"I'm waiting for an audience with the king. It's official business."

"I'm on official business, too. See you later." Then he added, "Good luck."

In a moment, Peter was summoned. He handed the inventory list to King Burger. "My name is Peter. The stable manager, Odibrand, asked me to deliver the horse inventory to you."

The king studied the list for what seemed like a long time. Peter had read the list and it wasn't that long. King Burger rubbed the short whiskers on his chin. "480? Is this accurate?"

"I believe so, sir. We did lose quite a few

horses in the attack on Mirabeau."

King Burger rose from his throne and began pacing the floor, deep in thought. "I want you to deliver a message back to Odibrand. And listen carefully. There can be no misunderstanding. Tell Odibrand, half of our war horses have gone lame."

"But, sir, only a couple dozen horses are lame and they aren't included in those numbers. Only horses fit for war were counted."

"Listen to me! Tell Odibrand, half of our war horses have gone lame and must be put down. I want that inventory number cut in half. Do I make myself clear?"

"If my lord wishes to reduce the inventory, perhaps he would sell the horses or even give them away to poor families in the city who would put them to good use and be forever grateful to their generous king."

"Silence! Half of the horses are to be put down. And someone will come to inspect on the day after tomorrow to see if it has been done. You are dismissed."

"It will be done," said Peter through clenched teeth.

That evening, the dining room was clean and freshly decorated. Ludwig was playing his violin in the corner. And the kitchen staff was serving a meal fit for a king and a king's guest. A young girl brought in the soup to start the meal.

"Grimbald," said King Burger, "to what do I owe the pleasure of your visit?"

Soup bowls fell to the floor with a clatter, but the two dignitaries barely noticed. She began mopping up the floor with the towel from the waist of her apron, while another servant went to get two more bowls of soup.

"King Burger, I'm here to make sure everything is ready, as you well know. This certainly isn't a social call. I'm here to make sure you've held up your end of our agreement—an agreement we paid you to keep, may I remind you?"

"Of course. Everything is going as planned. I'm taking care of a couple final details. I can provide evidence in the next couple days, if you wish to stay."

"Then the attack on Mirabeau may proceed without delay or hindrance?"

"Yes, according to our agreement."

"That's good because King Daggerhammer's army is on the move."

Alexandra picked up her towel, soaked with soup, and quietly left the dining hall.

Chapter 7
All the King's Horses

Peter raced back to the stable to tell Odibrand of the king's demand.

"That's troubling news, and a most unexpected turn of events," said Odibrand. "I think we should inform the army commanders." He left Peter at the stable and rode off to summon the officers.

The commanders arrived swiftly. Odibrand began with some introductions, "This is my new stable boy, Peter. And this is Sir Loin and Sir Cumference, commanders of the army. A few minutes ago, Peter returned from the castle with a dire message from the king. When King Burger saw today's inventory count of 480 war horses, he said—how did he put it, Peter?"

"He said half of our horses are lame and

must be put down."

"What?" exclaimed Sir Cumference.

"Wait a moment, does he mean we are to kill half of our war horses?" asked Sir Loin.

"I'm afraid so," said Odibrand.

Peter said, "Master, we can't put down half of the horses. That's 240 horses with a death sentence! We can't let that happen!"

"Calm yourself, son," said Sir Cumference.

Odibrand continued: "I don't see any other choice. If we don't kill the horses, the king will kill us for disobeying his command. You said it yourself: the king will send someone day after tomorrow to inspect our inventory to ensure compliance with his command."

Peter pleaded: "But, sir, there has to be something we can do. Could the army take them out of the city to hide them?"

"I'm not sure we could move 240 horses out of the city without notice," said Sir Loin, looking at Sir Cumference for confirmation.

"You're right," said Sir Cumference. "I can't think of any way—even if we divided them into small groups—to get them out without drawing too much attention. It's too bad there isn't a way to hide them in plain sight, somehow."

Suddenly Peter's eyes brightened. "I have an idea. Come with me." He darted off to the back of the stable. He kicked around in the straw, looking for something. "It looks like this hasn't been used in a while." Then he pulled a handle in the floor and opened a large hatch. He grabbed a lantern off a nearby post and led the way down a sturdy ramp.

Peter led the men through a long-forgotten underground stable, with stall after stall.

"What is this place?" asked Sir Cumference.

"And how did you know about it?" asked Odibrand.

"My guardian was the stable master for King Cole, so I grew up in the stables here. I knew a lot of secrets. King Cole wanted to keep some horses in a secret hiding place so if there was ever an emergency, he would have transportation for himself and his officers. Because there is no light down here, we rotated about a dozen horses every twelve hours."

"In the dark, I can't tell how big this is," said Sir Loin. "Are you suggesting we keep 240 horses down here?"

"It would be very crowded," said Peter, "but I think it could work for a couple days. We would still need to work out a way to rotate horses discreetly, but I think it can be done."

"Hmm," said Sir Cumference. "That's a good plan, but how would we convince the king's inspector that we have slaughtered the animals?"

Odibrand said, "I have about 20 lame horses that I've been trying to nurse back to health, but, truthfully, they will never be battle ready again. So, I wouldn't feel bad about putting them down. That would create sufficient mess to indicate a massive slaughter has taken place."

"I always hate to see animals slaughtered," said Sir Loin.

Just then Peter heard Alexandra in the stable calling his name. She sounded panicked. He ran up the ramp to see if she was okay and the men followed him.

"Peter—Peter—I," she was out of breath from running.

"Alex? Take a deep breath. Then tell me what's wrong. Is Sebastian in trouble?"

She shook her head.

"Peter, I overheard the king during his meal with someone named Grimbald, who seemed to be a messenger from King Daggerhammer of Cadence. King Burger has been paid by King Daggerhammer to do nothing to defend Mirabeau when Daggerhammer attacks again. Grimbald was sent to make sure everything was ready for the attack because King Daggerhammer is on the move."

The men all gasped.

"What?"

"How dare he!"

"King Daggerhammer is on the move? We don't have much time!"

"That explains why he wanted to reduce the number of horses available for battle."

"I can't believe he sold out his own throne for money. What kind of a king is he?"

When the emotions settled down a bit, Sir Cumference said, "Peter, I believe your plan to hide the horses below will work because it won't be very long before we need them. Make it so."

"Sir?" asked Peter, looking at Sir Cumference.

"Yes?"

"Could you spare a horse and rider to deliver a message to King Arthur of The Magic Kingdom? I believe they will come to our aid if we can get a message to them."

"What makes you think so?"

"Have the messenger say: Sir Peter, Knight of the Round Table, needs your help in defending Mirabeau against the armies of King Daggerhammer of Cadence."

"You're a knight?" asked Sir Cumference in bewilderment.

"Yes, sir. It's a long story, but I have the sword to prove it." With that he went to a corner and pulled out his magic sword from behind some bales of hay.

"This is a story I must hear sometime, but I will do as you request. I can spare a rider for such an important message that inspires hope."

"I'd like to hear that story, too," said Odibrand. "You are full of surprises, young man."

Chapter 8
A Secret Mission

Peter worked late into the night making modifications to the underground horse stalls. He split each stall into two or three smaller stalls. It would be tight, but it would have to do. Then, under cover of darkness, he began moving horses to their underground refuge.

While he was working, he thought of something else that needed to be done. He woke up Donkey Oatie, who jolted upright and went "Hee haw."

"Shh," said Peter, "it's just me."

"Oh, and I was having such a good dream about being in a cave underground and pulling carrots out of the ceiling to eat. Lots and lots of carrots."

"Donkey Oatie, I have a secret mission for

you. Do you think you're up to a challenge?"

"A secret? I love secrets! What's the secret?"

"I need you to travel, as fast as possible, back to Dirt Brown and the seven giants. Can you find your way back to them?"

"Yes, of course I can. But that's a pretty boring secret."

"Listen up! I need you to tell the giants we need their help. King Daggerhammer is on the way to attack Mirabeau and the city walls are still destroyed from his last attack. We need the giants to lift the large chunks of rubble into a makeshift wall so we have some protection. Can you remember that?"

"Yes. Ding Kaggerhammer . . ."

"It's King Daggerhammer."

"Oh, yes, of course. Anyway a bad king is going to attack Mirabeau and we need the giants to lift big rocks to keep the big, bad wolf from blowing our house down."

"Donkey!"

"I got it. I was just messing with you. We need them to lift chunks of rubble to create a wall of debris to keep the bad king out."

"Good. Now I know it's still dark out, but can you get started? And travel as fast as you can. And please don't get distracted. This is very important. People's lives depend on it. I know you can do it, Donkey Oatie. Good luck."

Donkey Oatie set out in the dark. When he reached the farmlands outside the city, he began jumping at shadows. The full moon cast long shadows and everything looked eerie.

Then he crossed the creek and entered Tanglewood. He was mindful to steer clear of the tangled mess they had encountered before. He kept trotting along, singing every song he could think of to keep from feeling afraid of being out here all alone.

> Here we go 'round
> The bramble bush,
> The bramble bush,
> The bramble bush.
> Here we go 'round
> The bramble bush
> So early in the morning.

"Oh, that's no good. I'm afraid I'm going to get caught in the bramble bushes and never get out. Let me try another song."

> All around the cobbler's bench,
> The monkey chased the weasel;
> The monkey thought
> 'twas all good fun.
> Pop! Goes the weasel.

"No, that's no good either. I saw a monkey jump out of one of those musical boxes once. It scared me to death. I don't need a song that will make me jumpy. Oh! I know a good one—and one of my favorites!"

> The farmer in the dell
> The farmer in the dell
> Heigh-ho, the derry-o
> The farmer in the dell
>
> The farmer has a donkey
> The farmer has a donkey
> Heigh-ho, the derry-o
> The farmer has a donkey
>
> The donkey saves the day
> The donkey saves the day
> Heigh-ho, the derry-o
> The donkey saves the day

As the first light of dawn was brightening the sky, Donkey Oatie finally found the house. It took him three tries, but he'd never admit he was lost.

Lofty was the first one he saw.

"Hello, Donkey Oatie. What brings you all the way out here?"

"I have an urgent message for all of you from Peter."

"Well, you'd better come inside, then."

Dirt Brown and the seven giants—Lofty, Stinky, Grumble, Tiny, Tingle, Giggle, and Snort—all greeted him.

Once inside, the seven giants gathered around Donkey Oatie in the kitchen. He said, "Something sure smells good in here."

"We're fixing oatmeal. You are welcome to eat with us as soon as we've heard your news."

"News? Oh, yes, *that* news. Peter asked me to travel all night to bring you an urgent message."

"Yes?" prompted Stinky.

For some reason Donkey Oatie's mind was blank. All he could think about was warm oats. He'd never had warm oats before. He was obsessed with the idea. "Are you sure we couldn't eat first?"

"Well, I guess so, but I thought you said the matter was urgent," said Lofty.

"Urgent or not, we all have to eat."

"Very well."

Tingle began serving oatmeal into giant blue bowls. "Do you want some maple syrup on that?" asked Tiny.

"Oooh! Yes, please! I've never had syrup on my oats."

Tiny walked over to the window and pulled a lever which drained fresh maple syrup directly from the maple tree. Then he set the bowl before Donkey Oatie.

Donkey Oatie smelled the steam coming off the bowl because he wanted to remember this moment for the rest of his life. He finally stuck his mouth in the bowl and began eating.

He had always eaten oats in a feed bag, but hot oats in a bowl was taking food to a whole new level. And maple syrup was a new experience for him. It was sweet and sticky, but he thought it was the best smelling thing he had ever eaten.

Donkey Oatie finished his oatmeal very quickly and while he was waiting for the giants to finish their meal, he fell asleep. He didn't mean to, but his stomach was full of warm food for the first time in his life and it made him relaxed and sleepy.

When the giants finished, they tried to wake him, but he was sound asleep. They called his name. They shook him. They dragged him outside. And, finally, they poured a bucket of water on him.

"What?" said Donkey Oatie with a start. He jumped up and saw the giants. Suddenly, it seemed funny, so he started going, "Hee haw. Hee haw. Hee haw."

The sight of Donkey Oatie kicking around going "Hee haw" made Giggle and Snort begin to laugh. In fact, Snort laughed so hard he began to snort.

When Donkey Oatie finally settled down, Lofty said, "What is this urgent message you keep putting off?"

"Urgent message. Hmm." Donkey Oatie tried to clear the sleepiness out of his head. "Urgent message. Peter. Oh, yes, it's coming to me now."

"Well, what is it?" asked Stinky.

"Peter said that Dag Kinghammer. No, wait. Kag Dinghammer. That's not right. King Daggerhammer. Yes, King Daggerhammer is going to attack Mirabeau. The city walls are still destroyed from his last attack so the city is defenseless. Peter is asking you to come lift chunks of debris to stack them into a makeshift wall to provide a shifty wall, or something like that. Hmm. That doesn't sound right. At any rate, could you come help build some defenses out of debris?"

The giants looked at each other.

"We haven't been on a vacation in years," said Tingle.

"We could use some exercise," said Stinky.

"Oh, please, Lofty. Can we go?" asked Tiny.

"Well, you heard him. Peter is in trouble and needs our help. Let's go!" said Lofty.

"Great. What do I have to pack for a trip like this?" mumbled Grumble.

Giggle and Snort were so excited, they began to dance and laugh. And Snort laughed so hard he began to, well, you know—snort!

Chapter 9
Don't Hold a Grudge

Odibrand saw the men coming down the street and called, "Peter, come quickly." King Burger entered the stable yard with a man unfamiliar to Odibrand. The stranger wore a black robe and his face had sharp edges and harsh lines that made his eyes appear to sink into his face under a prominent brow.

"Your honor, it is a pleasure to welcome you. How may we serve you today?" said Odibrand.

The king paused to look around before speaking. Pointing to Peter, he said, "I gave this boy an order. I have come to see that my order has been carried out."

Odibrand chose his words carefully, especially since he knew nothing of this stranger. "Your honor, all the lame horses have been put down and, if I may speak freely, I can give you an updated count of war horses."

"You may speak. Grimbald has come to inspect our military readiness and advise us accordingly."

"Yes, sir. Our new count includes 240 horses ready for battle."

"And the others have been properly disposed?"

"If you would follow me behind the stable, you will see for yourself where I have slaughtered the lame animals."

They followed Odibrand a short distance and then out a barn door. A large area was stained with blood, including knives, buckets, and rags. The king seemed satisfied. No indication of satisfaction appeared on Grimbald's expressionless face, but he did nod slightly at the king.

"Very well, then," said King Burger. "You have done well. May we have a look around?"

"Yes, of course. Let me show you through the stables so you can see the fine horses at your disposal," said Odibrand.

Just then, Peter realized he only had one of his two geckos in his pocket. He began nervously looking around. He looked in his pocket again. *I have Hunch*, he thought. Then he saw the other gecko run across the straw on the floor and run up the leg of the man in black. Grimbald said, "What? I've never seen a gecko with a red glow. Look at this."

Peter knew what was about to happen. "Wait! Don't hold Grudge!" But as the words came out of his mouth, Grimbald picked up the gecko, which suddenly turned red-hot and burst into flame.

Grimbald yelled and threw the flaming gecko at the wall, where the gecko cooled and turned back to his normal green color. Grimbald shook his hands and was clearly in pain.

The king stepped toward Peter. "Are you responsible for this?"

"Let's go," said Grimbald.

"As you wish," said the king. And they left the stable and walked up the street to the castle.

"What was that?" asked Odibrand.

"I'm sorry. I normally have a gecko in each pocket. I have Hunch," he said, pulling his gecko named Hunch out of his pocket. But I've learned by now, never hold Grudge," he said, indicating the gecko on the wall, named Grudge. "When Grudge feels threatened, he turns red hot and bursts into flames. It's hazardous to hold Grudge. You'll get burned."

"I see. Very interesting."

When King Burger arrived back at the

castle, a messenger was waiting for him. "Yes? What is it?"

"My lord, there are giants in the city."

"Giants? What do you mean?"

"There are several humongous men—giants—lifting large chunks of rubble and stacking them to rebuild the wall ruined in the battle."

"Rebuilding the wall! That can't be!"

"From a southern window, you will see them for yourself, my lord."

King Burger ran to the window and gasped. Sure enough, there were several giants rebuilding the wall from the debris.

Grimbald said, "This cannot be allowed, Ham Burger. We had an agreement. If you want your full payment, you must put a stop to this."

Chapter 10
A Rock and a Hard Place

The seven giants—Lofty, Stinky, Grumble, Tiny, Tingle, Giggle, and Snort—were busy stacking large chunks of debris like building blocks. While they worked, they were singing a song that Donkey Oatie liked very much:

> There's a hole in the bucket,
> dear Tiny, dear Tiny,
> There's a hole in the bucket,
> dear Tiny, a hole.
> Then mend it, dear Grumble,
> dear Grumble, dear Grumble,
> Then mend it, dear Grumble,
> dear Grumble, then mend it.
>
> With what shall I mend it,
> dear Tiny, dear Tiny?

With what shall I mend it,
dear Tiny, with what?
With straw, dear Grumble,
dear Grumble, dear Grumble,
With straw, dear Grumble,
dear Grumble, with straw.

After they sang that several times, they adapted it to their actual working situation and sang:

There's a hole in the wall,
dear Tiny, dear Tiny,
There's a hole in the wall,
dear Tiny, a hole.
Then mend it, dear Grumble,
dear Grumble, dear Grumble,
Then mend it, dear Grumble,
dear Grumble, then mend it.

With what shall I mend it,
dear Tiny, dear Tiny?
With what shall I mend it,
dear Tiny, with what?
With straw, dear Grumble,
dear Grumble, dear Grumble,
With straw, dear Grumble,
dear Grumble, with straw.

They were having a jolly good time, for Donkey Oatie loved sing-a-longs and didn't have singing companions very often. All of a sudden the royal guards showed up with swords drawn. "Halt!"

The giants kept working and singing because they didn't realize the men were talking to them.

"Halt! Stop! Put your hands in the air."

The giants looked puzzled and put their huge hands over their heads. Giggle and Snort thought this might be a fun new game. Donkey Oatie, who was nearby, thought they looked silly with their hands in the air, as if it were some sort of exercise class. He ran out between the giants and the royal guards, going "Hee haw. Hee haw."

Then he began to jabber at the guards: "That reminds me of a storybook I read in which the cowboy sheriff arrested a bad guy and said, 'Reach for the stars.' It was a pretty nice book, but cowboy stories are just fantasies, you know. They didn't really happen."

"Shut up!" yelled one of the royal guards.

"By whose authority do you repair the wall?" said the leader.

"We need authority?" asked Donkey Oatie.

"We're just here to help clean up the mess," said Lofty.

"That's not allowed unless the king authorizes it and the king didn't authorize it."

"Well he should have," said Stinky. "It's been broken for many months. Why hasn't the king fixed the wall?"

"Shut up," said the same guard, who apparently only knew these two words.

The leader stepped forward as much as he dared approach these giants. "I'll ask you one more time. Who authorized you to work on the wall? Who told you to do it?"

"We were authorized by the king," said Donkey Oatie.

"I already told you, the king did not authorize these repairs."

"Oh, yes he did. King Peter sent for us to come lift these heavy stones," said Tingle.

"King Peter? There is no King Peter, only King Burger—King Ham Burger."

"Great. He doesn't even know who the real king is," said Grumble.

A guard waved his sword at Donkey Oatie and said, "Explain yourself."

"Well, you see, Peter is the son of King Cole, the rightful king of Mirabeau. He and his friends took this amazing journey and we met these giants a few months ago. So when . . ."

"Shut up," said the shut-up guard.

"Where is this Peter now?" asked the leader.

"Well, I don't know for sure. I haven't seen him since yesterday," said Donkey Oatie.

"Where was he then?"

"The last time I saw him, he was working at the royal stable," said Donkey Oatie.

"We'll check it out. But you are ordered to stop work or we will blow you to bits like this wall."

"Okay, then. That's a good reason. Let's go have dinner," said Donkey Oatie.

Chapter 11
Allies Meeting in Alleys

Sebastian met lots of interesting people in the castle. He made an effort to introduce himself to everyone so he could know who might be useful when the time came. Today he met a man in the courtyard delivering crates of food. "Hi, my name is Sebastian. What's your name?"

"I am Wendell—Sir Wendell, technically."

"What is a knight doing delivering supplies?"

"I served as knight under King Cole, but when King Burger took the throne, he doubted the loyalty of King Cole's knights so he had us removed and he established his own inner circle of knights. But I hear he didn't even trust them and had them all killed for treason."

"I can confirm the truth of that. I was

present when it happened," said Sebastian.

"I'm not the only one. There are six of King Cole's knights living in exile from their royal duties."

"Sir Wendell, are you able to gather these men quickly?"

"I believe so. They all still reside in the city. But if you are asking us to fight, I think we have lost the heart for it. We have no desire to serve a tyrant."

Sebastian spoke softly: "Another attack on Mirabeau is coming. King Daggerhammer is on the move and he paid King Burger to not defend the city. So, don't do it for the king. Do it for the people—your families and friends. Do it because it is the right thing to do. Please! I urge you to gather your fellow knights and go to the royal stable. Ask for Peter."

"Who is Peter?"

"He is the son of King Cole, your rightful king."

"There were rumors about a royal son, but none of us ever knew if they were true."

"They are true."

"I will gather the men. Thank you. You have given me great hope."

Peter was brushing down a horse when a group of men approached. Odibrand greeted them, "What can we do for you today, gentlemen?"

"We are looking for Peter," said Sir Wendell.

Peter froze in place for a moment, wondering if this was good or bad. Odibrand turned and motioned for Peter to come forward."

"I am Peter."

"I spoke to a lad named Sebastian. He told me you are the son of King Cole, the rightful king of Mirabeau. Is this true? Are you the son of King Cole?"

Peter hesitated, wondering if these were friends or foes. "Who wants to know?"

"We are the knights who served as King Cole's advisors. King Burger questioned our loyalty to him so he had us removed and he appointed his own knights. I am Sir Wendell. And if you are the son of King Cole, we are at your service."

"I am."

Odibrand said, "You are full of surprises. I have known you three days and every day you pull out an even bigger surprise."

After some brief introductions, a vigorous discussion began as Peter gave them a full report on the situation, including how King Burger had betrayed the people by selling out to King Daggerhammer. Then Peter explained about having to reduce the number of war horses and how they hid them rather than killing them.

A second group of men approached and

Odibrand greeted them. "How may we help you today?"

"We are looking for a boy named Peter," said the leader.

"Who wants to know?" asked Odibrand.

"We are the royal guards, sent by the king to arrest the boy, Peter."

Peter's new friends rose to form a wall in front of the guards. The guards drew their swords.

"Wait!" shouted Peter. Then, looking to his loyal knights, he said, "Not now. You have a more important battle to fight. I will go with them."

The knights looked astonished at the courage of this young boy. Sir Wendell said, "As you wish. Stand down, men."

The guards slapped iron cuffs on Peter's wrists.

"Is that really necessary?" asked Odibrand.

The guards said nothing and backed away with their prisoner. Once they were on the street, they sheathed their swords.

Sir Wendell said, "Such selfless sacrifice! He will make a great king."

Chapter 12
The Dark of Knight

Alexandra was clearing the dining room after dinner when she saw Peter go by. She ran to the doorway and saw him being led down the hall to the king's chamber. He had shackles on his hands.

She quickly deposited the dinnerware in the kitchen and excused herself for a few minutes. Then she ran back to the servant's quarters to find her brother. Sebastian was napping, but she woke him. "Peter's been arrested! He was taken in shackles to the king."

"Come on," said Sebastian as he slipped into his boots and grabbed his coat.

As they worked their way through the castle, Sebastian said, "You'd better return to your duties. As the king's courier, I have the freedom to enter the king's chamber without notice. I'll see what I can find out."

Sebastian slipped into the king's chamber and leaned against the wall by the doorway, hoping to go unnoticed.

Peter was surrounded by guards as if he were a violent criminal. King Burger was pacing back and forth like a caged animal, while the guards explained.

"When we stopped the giants from rebuilding, we asked by whose authority they were repairing the wall. A babbling donkey told us it was on the authority of the king. When we pressed him further, he told us this boy, Peter, is the son of King Cole. He is acting under the delusion that he is king, I guess. We brought him to you for judgment."

The king walked a circle around Peter, studying him carefully. He stopped in front of him and bent down to get face to face with him. "You said your father was the stable manager for King Cole."

"I said my *guardian* was the stable manager."

"I see. And did your guardian tell you that you were the son of King Cole?"

"No, I learned that later."

"From whom? Who put this lie into your head?"

"Lucas the Magician."

"Lucas the Magician? You've seen him?"

A guard cleared his throat and King

Burger looked up. "Sire, if I may? The more I look at this boy—well, I'm positive he is one of the children we caught listening in here the other day. He is one of the intruders we chased through the castle and courtyard but did not capture."

"Hmm. Is that so?"

Peter wasn't sure that was a real question so he said nothing.

King Burger said, "There is more than sufficient evidence to declare you a traitor to the kingdom. I would be justified in killing you right now but, because you have claimed to be king, I want to make a public example of you so others will not pretend to make themselves king. Take him to the tower!"

The king waved his hand as if sweeping Peter out of his sight. The guards grabbed Peter's arms and hauled him away. On the way out the door, Peter's eyes met Sebastian's tear-filled eyes. Neither spoke a word. The brief gaze said it all.

Sebastian followed from a distance to see where they would take Peter. They went up the spiral stairs to the bridge. Sebastian waited in the shadows as the guards marched Peter across the bridge walkway to the prison tower.

They disappeared inside for a minute and then the guards emerged back onto the bridge walkway. As the guards closed the iron door on Peter's prison cell, thunder clapped in an ominous sign of doom.

The giants, who had built a bonfire and made some soup for dinner, sat around discussing their dilemma.

"Peter asked us to rebuild the wall and that's what we need to do," said Tingle.

"The guards will blow us to bits if we do," mumbled Grumble.

Lofty said, "What if we rebuilt the wall during the night when they couldn't see us?"

"But they will hear the thud of the rocks as we stack them. Dropping boulders on other boulders isn't something you can keep quiet," said Stinky.

A heavy rain began to fall and they felt even more dismal. Then came a loud clap of thunder. Lofty held up his hand for them to stop talking. Then another clap of thunder.

Lofty smiled. "They won't hear the crash of the stones over the clash of the thunder. Hurry! Let's get back to work. Concentrate on the largest breaches in the wall first."

As soon as her kitchen duties were done for the night, Alexandra brought Peter some bread and cheese and slid it under the door to his prison cell in the tower.

"Thank you, Alex." He was silent as he took a bite. "Alex? I want you and Sebastian to take Donkey Oatie and go back to The Magic Kingdom where you'll be safe and happy. It's dangerous here with this tyrant on the throne." He paused. "They're going to kill me to make a public example of me so the people will fear the king. I don't want you to watch me die. I need to die knowing you'll be safe, Alex."

"Oh, Peter!"

He could hear her quietly sobbing on the other side of the door. He wished there was no iron door between them. He wished he could hold her hand, put an arm around her, or give her a hug. Talking through an iron door was a lousy way to say goodbye, especially when goodbye meant forever.

Another clap of thunder rolled through the sky like a giant boulder. Then came some lightning. Alexandra got up off the floor where she had been leaning against Peter's cell door. She took a few steps to a window and gasped at what she saw in the next flash of lightning.

"Peter! Do you have a window? Look out the window to the south. It's the giants! They're rebuilding the wall under cover of darkness. It's pouring down rain but they are stacking boulders. The sound of the thunder is covering the sound of their work. Bless their hearts! Peter, can you see it?"

Peter looked out from behind the bars on the window. The tower was one of the few points high enough to provide a view of the giants working. "Yes, Alex, I see them."

"Oh, Peter, don't give up. The giants aren't giving up. I'm not giving up on you. We'll find a way to get you out of here."

Chapter 13
The Trojan Donkey

"Okay, my two co-conspirators, settle down. Are you in place? Because there's a guard ahead." Donkey Oatie peeked over his shoulder to look for the two geckos, Grudge and Hunch.

"Ready!" said Hunch.

The two geckos were clinging to Donkey Oatie's tail, hoping to hide themselves enough not to be seen while Donkey Oatie smuggled them into the castle. They could have entered the castle as if they were rodents, but they didn't know where to go and it was a mighty big castle—and they were short on time.

The guard said, "Stop! What does a donkey think he's doing in the castle? No animals—especially stinky ones who aren't house trained."

Donkey Oatie sniffed himself. "I'm not stinky."

The guard approached Donkey Oatie and began to walk a circle around him, so the geckos got nervous, and, you got that right, Grudge began to glow. To keep from being seen by the guard, Grudge and Hunch had to keep circling around Donkey Oatie's body to stay on the opposite side from the guard.

"What? Hee hee haw!" said Donkey Oatie because he was ticklish with the geckos climbing across his backside and clinging to his left flank. He regained his composure and said, "I was here the other day. I sang and danced for King Burger and his audience." Then puffing out his chest, he said, "I am a royal minstrel."

"Hmm," said the guard, looking over the donkey. "It seems like I may have seen you then. But if I recall that incident, you were thrown out."

The geckos now circled across Donkey Oatie's chest and over to his right flank. Grudge was getting hot and Donkey Oatie wondered if he would burst into flames and they would all go up in smoke. But the more pressing problem was that it tickled something fierce.

"Hee hee haw! That's too funny! Thrown out? Hee hee haw! I beg your pardon. I was given a royal escort after the performance was finished. Hee hee—gasp—Hee haw! A donkey with my skills is a rare find—an endangered species worth protecting."

"Is that so?" said the guard, rubbing his chin. "Then let's see what you can do. Sing! Dance! Do your thing!"

The guard was directly in front of Donkey Oatie and Grudge and Hunch didn't know where to go so they crawled down onto his underbelly, where Donkey Oatie was even more ticklish.

"Sing? Hee hee, oh, hee haw!"

"That's it?"

"No. I'm just warming up. Hee hee hee haw!" Donkey Oatie wanted them off his belly so he began scratching with his hind leg and his hoof would hit the floor each time.

"Is that your dance?"

"You really don't know much about musicians, do you?" said Donkey Oatie, stalling for time. "I was just getting the beat for my song. Okay, I'll sing one I wrote for Alexandra, the new girl who works in the royal kitchen." The geckos were back in his tail now, so he felt more confident singing and dancing for his audience.

> Oh, have you seen my muffin pan,
> My muffin pan, my muffin pan?
> Have you seen my muffin pan?
> Did it go down the drain?

Oh, yes, I've seen your muffin pan,
Your muffin pan, your muffin pan.
Here, I've got your muffin pan,
I made your muffins plain.

Oh, thank you for my muffin pan,
My muffin pan, my muffin pan.
Thank you for my muffin pan,
I've got muffins on my brain.

As he was singing, Donkey Oatie swayed and crossed his feet as he side-stepped back and forth to each line. His tail was swinging back and forth and he worried that a gecko would go flying across the room at any moment.

When Donkey Oatie finished his act, he looked up at the guard with a big donkey grin. The guard had a smirk on his face and said, "Very well, if the king wants a singing, dancing donkey in the castle, who am I to say no?"

"Thank you very much, sir. I'll see you around." Then Donkey Oatie cleared his throat to tell Grudge and Hunch to relocate before he put his backside to the guard to walk down the hall.

Grudge and Hunch crawled across his underbelly and Donkey Oatie stifled another "Hee haw." Then they crawled up on his chest and out of sight of the guard as Donkey Oatie turned his backside to the guard.

Once they were a safe distance up the hallway, Donkey Oatie said, "Now that was awkward. Here I was trying to win a singing competition and I felt like I had ants in my pants with you two tickling my belly. And Grudge, you'd better be cool, little dude, because I don't want a gecko-shaped brand mark on my backside."

Grudge said, "I was just trying to light a fire under your singing career." Grudge and Hunch snickered but Donkey Oatie rolled his eyes.

After navigating various halls and stairways, Donkey Oatie brought them out on the bridge to the prison tower. There were no guards nearby because the prison tower was considered so secure. Donkey Oatie trotted across the bridge to the iron door.

A clap of thunder rolled through the night air.

"Peter? You in there?" asked Donkey Oatie.

"Donkey Oatie? What are you doing here?"

"Sebastian and Alexandra told me you were in prison here. We couldn't stand the thought of you being alone all night so I brought you a couple of cellmates." Grudge and Hunch crawled under the door.

"Oh, hello, guys," said Peter. Grudge was

glowing hot when he came under the door and he immediately burst into flames all over his body. "Thanks for bringing me a light—and heat, Donkey Oatie."

"Well, I'd say it was my pleasure, but I need to go check myself. I think I have a gecko-shaped brand mark on my backside."

"Oops! Well, you could start a fashion trend with that. You could tell people you wear the mark of the dragon because you fought the dragon."

"Peter, *you* fought the dragon while I hid in the bushes, remember?" Peter laughed. Donkey Oatie continued: "You should know by now: I laugh in the face of danger and then I hide until it goes away. I live longer that way."

"Well, you helped get Sebastian and Alexandra out of danger when they were injured by the dragon," Peter reminded him.

"Now I wish I could get *you* out of danger."

"Thanks, Donkey Oatie."

Another clap of thunder filled the silence as they all contemplated Peter's fate tomorrow.

Donkey Oatie cleared his throat and said, "Alright, boys, get to work!"

"Get to work?" said Peter through the heavy door.

"Sebastian and Alexandra thought they might be the keys to getting you out of here."

The two geckos crawled up the door and began exploring front and back to discover how it was locked and what might be done about it. Hunch searched one side and Grudge searched the other side of the door.

There was a large key hole on the outside of the door. Donkey Oatie held Hunch on his snout so the gecko could stick his tail in the key hole and dig around. It was a longshot but maybe, with a little luck, Hunch would be able to move the tumblers with his tail.

"They're very heavy. I'm not sure I can make it budge," said Hunch. "I'll keep trying. Ouch! No, my tail isn't strong enough to move the mechanisms where they need to be. I'm sorry. If it were a smaller lock, maybe, but this is too heavy."

Grudge gave it a try, too, but with the same result.

Peter said, "You guys had a good idea. You tried, but it's not your fault. I appreciate the effort. Actually, I appreciate all three of you. Have a good life if I don't make it."

"You're not dead yet," said Donkey Oatie.

The thunder rolled again.

Chapter 14
The Attack of Yogi Ogre

At first light, soldiers went through the city, gathering up all townsfolk. The people gathered in the town square, as was custom when the king wanted to speak to the people.

Peter woke to the sound of a large crowd of people. He looked out the small, barred window from his cell at the top of the prison tower.

Guards opened his cell door with a bang. Two burly men grabbed him by the arms and led him across the long narrow bridge that connected the prison tower to the castle. Peter could see the restless crowd.

The guards led Peter down some stairs and across the courtyard. Then they dragged him up onto a platform above the crowd, where they chained him to a post.

The soldiers cleared the inner courtyard, pushing the crowd back to form a wall of people around the perimeter.

King Burger entered a second platform to Peter's right. The crowd grew silent. The king addressed the crowd:

"This boy, Peter, has claimed to be king of Mirabeau."

The crowd laughed. The king nodded and some guards pushed Sebastian and Alexandra out into the cleared area of the courtyard.

"No!" cried Peter.

The king continued: "And his two friends are co-conspirators. The three of them were caught as intruders in the king's chamber and they initially evaded the guards. Then they had the nerve to infiltrate the castle staff as valets to gain access to the king's secret dealings. They are traitors to their king and deserve death. I bring them before you so you will know that traitors will be dealt with most severely."

A guard began to turn a crank, raising the large barred gate in the holding area below the prison-tower bridge. Before the gate was completely open, a large creature bowed its head and ducked under the gate to get out. When it stood up straight, it was a huge, hideous ogre, with slime dripping off its body.

King Burger said, "Before I kill the boy

who would be king, I'm going to make him watch his friends die in a mortal combat with the legendary Ogre of Yogurt."

The crowd gasped in one collective breath.

The ogre was disoriented a moment with so many people around, but a guard poked him in the rear with a spear. The ogre rubbed his rear end and stumbled forward a few steps, where he noticed Sebastian and Alexandra.

Sebastian pushed his sister back. "Look around the crowd for a familiar face, Alex. When the ogre attacks me, dash into the crowd and perhaps someone will help you escape unharmed."

Alexandra said, "I'm not leaving you here to die!"

"Alex, if you don't leave, we will both die."

The ogre took some lumbering steps that might have been considered running. He reached down to swipe at the kids but they both darted out of harm's way.

The slimy beast reached for them again, but they ran between its giant legs. The ogre bent forward to look between its legs and saw the kids. He turned to face them.

As he began to make a big, sweeping grab for them, Sebastian said, "Alex, stop, drop, and roll." Both kids dropped to the ground and rolled out of the ogre's reach.

While Alexandra was getting to her feet, the ogre grabbed her from behind. He picked her up and held her high in the air. The crowd gasped and some of the women screamed.

Sebastian's heart was beating hard. He walked up to the ogre and kicked him in the leg. "Hey, let her go! If you want a new toy, take me! Besides, girls have cooties!"

He knew if they survived this, he'd hear about that last statement, but he needed to get the ogre's attention.

The ogre dropped Alexandra and she went "uff" as she hit the ground. Then she rolled away—at least out of the ogre's reach for now.

Sebastian said, "Alex, get out of here fast!"

"Not without you!" she yelled as she got up.

"Alex, I'm telling you, if you don't leave, we will both die!"

"I hate it when there are no good choices," said Donkey Oatie. He trotted to the center of the arena and right up to the ogre. "Phew! You stink! What do they call you? Stinky?"

The ogre smiled at this new distraction. His teeth were grungy gray, but I suppose if you're an ogre, you don't brush your teeth.

"My name is Yogi Ogre." The ogre put his hands on his knees and bent down to look at the cute donkey.

"Yogi Ogre? What kind of name is Yogi Ogre? It sounds like something out of a song. Here's a little taunt-song for you:"

> Yogi Ogre was no bear.
> Yogi Ogre had no hair.
> Yogi Ogre was very ugly
> Wasn't he?

Yogi Ogre was amused with this toy donkey.

"Where does an ogre come from, anyway?" asked Donkey Oatie.

"I am from the Land of Yogurt."

"What's yogurt?" asked Donkey Oatie.

"It's sort of like a thick, gooey swamp where I live. But it comes in delicious flavors and I like it so much I take a bath in it."

"I guess that explains the gooey slime dripping off. You know, you really ought to get a towel to wipe yourself off after your bath. Wait! Did you say flavors? As in edible?"

"Yes, yogurt is delicious. You can lick my leg if you would like to taste it."

"I am *not* going to lick your leg."

"Oh, come on. Try it. You'll like it," taunted Yogi Ogre.

Donkey Oatie had multiple reasons to be skeptical, but he also had an uncontrollable love for food. He stepped forward very slowly, pausing from time to time. Then he reached out his neck and quickly licked the ogre's leg.

"Oooh! It tastes like strawberries. I love strawberries!" Then he stepped closer and licked again—and again. In fact, Donkey Oatie kept licking because this was a very tasty ogre.

"That tickles," said Yogi Ogre. "Oh, stop. It tickles!"

Donkey Oatie kept licking the yogurt.

"I can't stand it. It tickles—oh!" Yogi Ogre started laughing and he laughed so hard he fell on the ground with a huge thud.

The crowd of onlookers wasn't sure what to make of all this. Had they been brought here to watch an execution or a freak show?

Then Donkey Oatie got up on the ogre's belly and began licking some more. "Up here it tastes like blueberries!"

Yogi Ogre was laughing and kicking and throwing his arms around in hysterical laughter. The crowd of people looked on in astonished silence. King Burger said, "Guards! Do something!"

The guards looked at each other, not sure what the king meant they should do.

Sebastian and Alexandra took advantage of the momentary chaos and climbed up the stairs to the platform where Peter was chained up. "Peter, I don't have the keys. I don't know how to get you lose," said Sebastian.

"Is there a way to pull the post out of the

platform? How is it attached?" asked Peter.

"Hey, you!" yelled one of the guards, who suddenly realized what was happening.

Peter said, "Both of you get out of here! There will be another opportunity. Go!"

"I think he might be right, Alex." Sebastian took Alexandra's hand and they leapt off the side of the platform and hit the ground running. They kept running and running until they were out of breath and they stopped to hide under some stairs.

Chapter 15
Assassin Bugs

In the chaos, King Burger had disappeared back into the castle. The crowds pressed back into the courtyard and guards tried to control them. Peter stood chained to the post on the platform, watching Donkey Oatie lick a giant ogre, who was laughing and kicking rather than destroying his intended prey: Sebastian and Alexandra. If the situation were not so dire, Peter would have laughed.

With so much going on, everyone was startled to hear cannon fire strike the city wall. The crowd stood in stunned silence, not sure what was happening. Even the ground shook underneath them.

When the smoke began to clear, a wave of motion appeared over a breach in the wall. Everyone strained to see through the smoke. It was a swarm of very large insects. Dozens of them scurried over the wall and then it became hundreds. "Assassin Bugs!" shouted a man in the crowd.

The Assassin Bugs were the size of a dinner plate. They made a rather intimidating screeching sound, which was amplified by the sheer quantity of them.

The crowd of people was pressed up against the castle, with the Assassin Bugs blocking their escape to the roads home. The people were in danger of trampling each other as they tried to press into the crowd to get away from the deadly bugs.

The swarm of bugs reached the people and Peter watched in helpless horror. The Assassin Bugs would stab a person to inject deadly saliva and, instantly, the person would fall down. The saliva liquefied their insides and then the Assassin Bugs would suck out their insides. Peter yanked against his chains to no effect.

Just then, the seven giants stepped over the wall. All seven of them began a harmonic hum that grew louder and softer in pulses of soothing sound. The Assassin Bugs stopped what they were doing. For a moment they seemed confused, and then they fell asleep.

Peter recalled that the giants tended animals so they knew how to put the bugs to sleep with that harmonic hum.

The giants approached the crowd and people began to scream until the giants unfurled large burlap bags and started filling them with Assassin Bugs.

Then one man in the crowd yelled, "The giants attacked us with their bugs!"

King Burger stepped back onto the platform and shouted: "Guards! Attack the giants! Bugler! Summon the army!" The piercing tone of the bugle rang through the air.

The palace guards drew their swords and approached the giants, but they seemed to recognize the futility of whacking a giant in the knee. The giants ignored the pesky guards and continued gathering the Assassin Bugs. They made quick work of it and looked around to see if they had missed any. Three or four people pointed out bugs that still needed to be collected.

Just as they had arrived, the giants stepped over the wall with their bags of bugs. As they did, cannon fire tore through the wall near them. Grumble got struck by some flying debris and fell down. Tiny and Tingle helped him to his feet and got him out of there.

The crowd was beginning to break up as people began to move toward the street to go home. More cannon fire came near the entrance of the courtyard so people backed away from the exit in uncertainty.

With the L-shaped castle framing the courtyard to the north and west, and the wall under attack to the south, the people began moving to the east to escape. Then King Burger's army approached and formed a line of infantry and cavalry on the east. Some people tried to walk through the king's soldiers but were blocked and pressed back. The people were pinned in on all sides.

King Burger had the slightest smile of grim satisfaction.

Chapter 16
Start Wars

"Hey, let us through!" yelled one citizen.

"The enemy is to the south!" yelled another.

"Out of our way!"

"Get us out of here!"

One of the citizens in the courtyard yelled, "It's a trap!" People began to panic, looking for a way out.

The crowd became frantic as they began to realize the king's army wasn't for the people; they were against the people.

"What's the meaning of this?" someone yelled.

"King Burger, are you out of your mind? The armies of Cadence are on our doorstep!"

"King Daggerhammer will kill us all if you don't do something!"

The crowds began to press into the infantry, but were met with the edge of blades. The crowd backed off for a moment and then surged forward again. The soldiers struck down many of their own citizens at the front of the crowd. Then the horse-mounted soldiers of the cavalry pressed in to re-enforce the line.

The swordsmen continued to beat back the citizens and the enemy's cannons continued to assault the wall and nearby areas. Each cannon fire caused an eruption of screams from the crowd gathered in the courtyard.

Peter jerked on his chains, although he knew it was useless.

Now there was a breach in the wall sufficient for King Daggerhammer's troops to start pouring through on foot and on horseback. The people in the courtyard began to scream again.

Peter rattled his chains in frustration because he was afraid he was going to stand here chained to the post and have to watch his people get slaughtered. He screamed, "Nooooo!" Then he began to jerk on his chains again.

"Peter!" yelled Alexandra, who was peeking over the edge of the platform on his left. "I have a Hunch everything will work out." Then she rolled a ball across the platform. It bumped against Peter's feet and unfurled into a gecko.

"Hunch!" said Peter, who just now understood Alexandra's meaning. Then the gecko climbed up the post where Peter's hands were chained behind his back. Peter held out his hands like a shelf and Hunch sat on his hands while he poked his pointy tail into the keyhole and wiggled it around. "Click!" And then a few seconds later, "Click!"

"You're free," said Hunch.

Alexandra and Sebastian had climbed up on the platform with Peter by now. Just then a huge crash occurred just east of the courtyard. People screamed.

"Whoa! What was that?" asked Alexandra.

"It was a UFO," said Sebastian.

"A UFO?" asked Alexandra.

"An unidentified flying object—UFO," explained Sebastian.

"They've set up catapults. The enemy is hurling chunks of our own wall at us, Alex." Peter looked at Sebastian. "Really, Sebastian. What kind of books have you been reading?"

"It's called science fiction, but I think it's more science than fiction." Sebastian slapped Peter on the shoulder and said, "Peter, we brought your sword from the stable and look who else we found there!"

Sir Wendell sat in full armor on his horse and he was accompanied by 239 other horsemen loyal to the heir of King Cole. Not all of them wore armor, but their loyalty made up for the lack of armor.

"Men of Mirabeau!" shouted Sir Wendell. He rode in front of King Burger's army and continued, "Don't fight each other! Don't fight for King Burger. Fight for Mirabeau! Join your brothers and fight against a common foe. Fight against all who make themselves enemies of Mirabeau!"

King Burger's men seemed confused. Apparently, they didn't understand why there were two armies. In the confusion, King Daggerhammer's men advanced into the courtyard area, with swords drawn.

"Attack the army of Cadence!" shouted Sir Wendell. "Save Mirabeau! Charge!"

King Burger yelled, "Don't listen to him! I order you to hold your position and contain the people. Disobey me and you will be killed as a traitor!"

Sir Wendell yelled, "He is the traitor. He sold out Mirabeau to King Daggerhammer. He is an enemy of Mirabeau.

In the ensuing chaos of horses and humans, it became difficult to know what exactly was going on.

Peter fastened his sword to his waist and leapt off the platform. He scrambled up to King Burger's platform and, before the king realized it, Peter had pointed a blade at his head. "Call off your men," said Peter. The king did nothing. "Now!" yelled Peter.

The king stepped forward as if he were about to address the crowd. Then he swung around with sword drawn and Peter barely blocked it in time. "You have defied me for the last time," said King Burger as they held their swords against each other.

Peter broke away and took a swing at the king. When his blade struck the king's blade, Peter's blade began to glow blue.

The chaos in the courtyard escalated. Soldiers fought soldiers, with even neighbors and friends fighting against one another. The small band of soldiers led by Peter's friend, Sir Wendell, was stretched thin, with most of them defending the breach in the wall to slow down the progress of King Daggerhammer's armies. But with King Burger's men attacking their own people, some of Sir Wendell's men had to try to save innocent lives.

In the midst of the chaos, Sir Cumference saw a piece of wood fly through the air so he looked to see where it came from. Chuck the Woodchuck was chucking wood at enemy soldiers. Sir Cumference said, "Remind me to have you knighted when this is over, my little friend."

As Sir Cumference returned his attention to the battle, he saw fighting in groups all over the place. The whipping sound of swords slashing through the air until they clashed against each other could be heard above the yelling, screams, and clamor.

Then, someone in the crowd yelled, "His sword! Look at his sword! It glows blue!"

Peter continued to duel with King Burger, but he was aware of a group of people stopping to watch the unlikely match between a boy and a king.

Alexandra raced through the castle. She had grabbed as many arrows as she could carry from the armory and was headed for an upper balcony when the king's steward, Myles, stopped her. "Where are you headed, young lady?"

"I'm headed for a balcony to strike the enemy with arrows. Excuse me, I'm in a hurry."

"What can you do? You're just a girl. Go with the women and children who are hiding in the lower levels of the castle." He pointed to the stairs at the end of the hallway.

"What can I do? I've fought a dragon before! There's plenty I can do."

Myles patted her on the head and smiled. "Run along, my dear, before you get hurt."

She ran the direction he was sending her, but then she doubled back and made it to the upper balcony. Alexandra readied her bow for action. She focused on those soldiers who were harming unarmed citizens. Sometimes she had to be careful not to hit an unarmed citizen who might be struggling against a soldier. But her aim was true.

Ready. Aim. Whoosh.

There were plenty of targets to choose from.

Ready. Aim. Whoosh.

She felt sadness for all those who were being harmed.

Ready. Aim. Whoosh.

But her sadness was overcome by anger at those who would do such a thing.

Ready. Aim. Whoosh.

Alexandra was hitting nearly everything she aimed at. An occasional arrow deflected off of armor but she always hit her mark. She had taken down many of the enemy soldiers. And she still had a good supply of arrows.

Sebastian had grabbed a horse whose rider had been slain. He rode to the front line to help defend the wall. It was difficult to maneuver the horse with all the debris near the wall, but he got in there with his fellow horsemen and followed their lead.

King Daggerhammer's men wore full coats of armor, so it was difficult to make a fatal blow, but knocking them down was a good start. The soldiers had great difficulty getting up because of the weight of the armor. Soldiers on foot tried to land a fatal blow on them while they were down, but, with all the chaos and shortage of soldiers, a number of Daggerhammer's men were getting through.

Suddenly, Sir Wendell shouted, "Retreat! Retreat! We're being overrun! Retreat! Fall back to the courtyard! Retreat!"

"Peter! Help! Peter!" yelled Alexandra.

Peter could hear her on the balcony above him. It sounded like a scuffle as she struggled with someone.

Peter dropped his sword arm and punched King Burger in the stomach. "Later!"

The king doubled over at the unexpected blow and Peter ran off the platform and into the castle to look for Alexandra. He ran up a flight of stairs and met a man with Alex slung over his shoulder. She wasn't moving.

Peter landed a side-arm swing of his sword into the man's mid-section. The man fell forward onto Peter and all three bodies tumbled down the stairs. Peter struggled to get out from under the heavy man. Then he unfolded Alexandra, who was crumpled up in a heap.

He rolled her over and saw her eyes flutter. "Alex? Alex? Are you okay? Are you injured?" He began checking her body for signs of blood and he felt her arms and legs for broken bones. "Alex? Talk to me. Are you okay?"

"Peter, I'm here." She coughed a couple times.

"What happened?" asked Peter.

"I was shooting arrows. He grabbed me from behind. We struggled. Then I think he drugged me when he put his hand over my nose and mouth. Or I just passed out from fear. But I feel weird now, so I think he drugged me."

"Could be. Are you okay now? I've got a king to catch."

"I'm fine. Thanks for coming for me. Now, go!"

"I'm glad you're okay, Alex." Then he turned and ran off to look for King Burger.

Alex ran back up the stairs to her bow and arrows on the balcony.

When Peter returned to the king's platform, what he saw made him step back behind the curtain. King Burger was speaking to another man even more lavishly robed and richly adorned with gold jewelry around his neck and wrists.

"King Daggerhammer, you're here sooner than expected," said King Burger.

"Thank you. That was the easiest invasion ever. You upheld your end of our bargain by limiting resistance." King Daggerhammer reached out his right hand to shake hands with King Burger, but while their hands were clasped, he used his left hand to thrust a dagger into King Burger's belly. "Too bad I won't be upholding my end of our bargain. I changed my mind. I don't want to settle for pillaging the city for wealth. I want to be king after all."

Shocked at the betrayal and at being stabbed, King Burger held his stomach and fell to his knees. After a few seconds of kneeling there with his mouth open, King Daggerhammer pushed him over backwards and he fell to the ground where he died— just a couple feet away from where Peter stood watching.

A lot of the fighting had stopped as King Daggerhammer had entered the city so a crowd was forming before the platform. King Daggerhammer held up his arms for attention and said:

"Citizens of Mirabeau, I am King Daggerhammer of Cadence. I know I attacked your city a few months ago, but when I heard King Burger had made himself a king with a tyrannical reign, I had to return. I had learned that Burger intended to slaughter his own people so I came to liberate you—and I have! King Burger is dead by my own hand. He cannot terrorize you again."

There were muffled cheers among the crowd. People were stunned and skeptical about what all this meant.

"King Burger's army has been slaughtering your citizens today. For your own safety, I am going to detain you in the castle while we sort out these rogue soldiers from among your ranks."

"No!"

"You can't do that!"

"You have no right!"

"Oh, yes, I do have the right. I am your new king! Soldiers! Lock up these citizens in the holding area under the west bridge. If anyone gives you trouble, put him in the tower."

People began to be herded like cattle through the gate from which the ogre had emerged.

Peter, still behind the curtain, could hear the screams and cries of "Help!" from his people. He clutched his sword, wondering what to do about this unexpected turn of events. King Daggerhammer was a few feet away on the platform outside.

Sebastian had gone upstairs to get Alexandra after hearing her earlier cries for help. Now the two of them stood across the room, motioning for Peter to come with them. Peter stood still and peeked out the doorway once more. He hesitated while trying to decide what to do and then he joined his friends.

"Peter, let's go. We can regroup with Sir Wendell and anyone left to come up with a unified plan," said Sebastian.

Peter shook his head. "King Daggerhammer is relatively unguarded at the moment. I think I should confront him now."

Alexandra reached out and put her palm against Peter's chest. "Peter, stop a moment. Just rest. Breathe." He felt as though a warm, relaxing heat flowed through his body. He slumped to the floor in exhaustion.

"So many people have died," said Peter. "It's difficult to watch. This isn't what I expected."

"What did you expect?" asked Sebastian.

"I don't know. Not this. Not war. Not multiple kings fighting for control. Not widespread death and bloodshed."

"I know. It's sad. It's overwhelming to everyone," said Alexandra.

"I wish Lucas the Magician were here. He'd know what to do. Or even King Arthur. He could act with authority."

Sebastian looked his friend in the eyes and said: "But *you* are the king, Peter. You know what must be done. Do you have the courage to do it? Are you ready to *be* the king?"

Chapter 17
Verbal Swordplay

Peter, Sebastian, and Alexandra made a plan and went their separate ways. Peter hoped Sebastian could round up the right men, but he was more concerned about whether Alexandra could carry out her part of the plan. However, there was no time to worry now. He had to do his part to occupy King Daggerhammer while the others got in place.

Peter noticed some of King Daggerhammer's men had gone into the royal chambers and hauled the enormous throne out onto the platform. It was at least ten feet tall and almost as wide, adorned with jewels, etchings, and decorative paintwork.

King Daggerhammer was seated upon the throne, making quite a spectacle of himself while soldiers continued to gather up citizens. Small skirmishes and outbursts occurred here and there, but Daggerhammer's men quickly settled the matter—usually at the end of a sword.

Peter was concerned because the will of the people was breaking and they were not resisting as much as they had at first.

After taking a deep breath, Peter stepped out from the castle onto the platform, behind the throne. As he came around the throne, two soldiers saw him and leapt forward to block his way by crossing two spears in front of him. He didn't feel threatened, just annoyed. He pushed them aside and spoke directly to King Daggerhammer while the two soldiers hesitated to get aggressive with a boy.

"King Daggerhammer, you have no authority here!" stated Peter in a loud voice, hoping to draw attention.

The king and his soldiers laughed.

"That's very brave of you, boy. Now run along."

"After you," said Peter, extending his arms to point the way down the stairs off the platform.

They chuckled again. "You're amusing, but we don't have time."

Then, raising his voice, Peter said: "I said you have no authority here!" People nearby—including soldiers of various armies—began to look his direction to see what was happening.

"What would you know? You're just a child! I am king. Of course I have authority here."

"You made yourself king!" shouted Peter.

"Are you going to challenge me?"

"I defy you! We will not submit to you," said Peter with a strong, authoritative voice. He knew he had to inspire the people of Mirabeau to fight against the enemies.

King Daggerhammer waved his arm to point to the containment area and said, "Apparently your people already have submitted to me."

"Not for long," said Peter, "Now stand down!"

"You're quite impressive for a boy your age. I'd like to recruit you for an exalted position in my kingdom. Let's talk about where you would like to serve."

"You're not listening. I'm not going to serve you. None of us are willing to serve you. Stand down!"

"How dare you speak to your king that way! You're just a boy, so I'm willing to overlook the matter if you run along now."

"You will stand down from asserting yourself as king."

"Is that a threat? What are you going to do to stop me?"

"That wasn't a threat, but this is: You will

stand down at once—or you will die."

"You? Kill a king?" King Daggerhammer and his soldiers laughed again. Much of the fighting in the courtyard area stopped and people drew nearer to watch this drama unfold.

"This is not a joke. I don't know what you find so amusing. I defeated the dragon of Magic Mountain and I defeated the evil sorcerer, Deofol. I can defeat you, too."

"You did no such thing! You're making up stories. All boys fancy themselves as dragon slayers."

"But I really did slay the dragon."

"I doubt it."

"Then you shouldn't be afraid to fight me." Peter drew his sword from the sheath and realized it was already glowing in the sheath. *Hmm. It's never done that before*, thought Peter.

The two soldiers stepped in front of the king, but King Daggerhammer's eyes were bulging with rage as he pushed past them.

"You varmint! I was going to spare you since you're just a boy. I even considered offering you a position in my kingdom. But I cannot let a direct challenge go unmet. You have guts, kid, but they're about to get you gutted." The king drew his sword.

A large crowd—mostly soldiers for various kings—had gathered as this verbal challenge had escalated.

Chapter 18
The Dual Duel

Sebastian had gone to find some of the knights, only to run across them gathered at the east entrance of the castle. Sir Wendell said, "Sebastian! We're glad to see you're safe."

"I just conferred with Peter. He has a plan to regroup," said Sebastian.

"Excellent. That's what we were just discussing," said Sir Loin.

"We need to get the people to fight for themselves, but they need us to lead the way. Peter is going to occupy the attention of King Daggerhammer. Sir Wendell, we need you to work on setting the captives free. Alexandra is working on rounding up some big help for you, but you can't wait for her. Do what you can."

"Yes, sir. I should be able to get up to the

gate. Getting it open might take some creativity," responded Sir Wendell.

"Do the best you can. Sir Cumference, have your men form a perimeter around the courtyard, including the occupying troops. We need to contain the battle and destroy any enemy who tries to retreat."

"That shouldn't be a problem, sir," said Sir Cumference.

Sebastian smiled. "You guys don't have to call me 'sir.' I'm not a knight."

"You will be soon, sir," said Sir Wendell.

Sebastian continued: "Sir Loin, with a perimeter established, we need you to lead your men against the enemy. Confront them directly, or drive them back to the perimeter where your brothers can back you up. This will be the bloodiest part of any of the assignments."

"We're ready to give life and limb," said Sir Loin.

Sebastian looked at the remaining knight. "I'm sorry. I don't believe we've met. I'm Sebastian."

"Greetings, young sir. I'm Sir Valence."

"Sir Valence, I need you and your men to be our eyes and ears. Keep an eye on troop movements, especially if any enemies retreat into the castle, escape beyond the perimeter, try to infiltrate the city, or manage to regroup in any way that we need to be warned about."

"Yes, sir. We can do that. I'll have some foot soldiers sweep the castle for enemies and then guard the entrances. My mounted troops can patrol the outlying areas for enemy activity."

"Great!" said Sebastian. "Good luck, men. I've got to run!"

Sebastian ran back up the stairs of the castle to check on Peter. On the landing at the top of the stairs was the hooded man in black—Grimbald!

Grimbald had been nervously wringing his hands while he stood watching King Daggerhammer on the platform as he was confronted by the stable boy, Peter.

Sebastian approached Grimbald cautiously and uttered his name: "Grimbald." The man jumped because he was previously unaware of Sebastian's presence.

Sebastian held his sword at his side, but he decided to take another strategy. "You were sent here by King Daggerhammer. What was your purpose here?"

Grimbald showed his blackened teeth in what might have been a smile. "I was to make sure King Burger made preparations that would allow King Daggerhammer to easily take the kingdom."

"What do you mean? Why would King Burger give up the throne?"

"Oh, he didn't know he was giving up the

throne. He agreed to make it easy for King Daggerhammer to pillage and plunder the city. Then Burger would pretend to drive out the invaders, making him look like a hero. Daggerhammer would get the looted wealth and Burger would get a boost in public support."

"You're kidding."

"No. It's true. But Burger didn't know King Daggerhammer's true intentions. With the city's defenses softened, King Daggerhammer could conquer Mirabeau with ease, kill King Burger, and take the throne for himself."

"Why are you telling me this so willingly? What's your game?" asked Sebastian.

"No game. I wanted to brag about my master plan before I kill you." Grimbald whipped a dagger out of his cloak and hurled it at Sebastian.

Sebastian had his sword in hand, although it hung at his side during their discussion because he didn't want to provoke Grimbald. Now he ducked out of the way of the flying blade, but it was close. Sebastian readied his sword.

Grimbald took off running up the next flight of stairs. Sebastian followed. When he rounded the corner at the top, Grimbald was standing there holding a sword. Sebastian didn't hesitate. He lunged at Grimbald and the two began to fight vigorously.

Their footwork carried them across the room in a series of quick-action blows. Then they clashed blades in a doorway and Sebastian managed to back Grimbald out onto a balcony. Sebastian had him cornered now, hopefully.

"Donkey Oatie," said Alexandra when she finally found him. "Oh, my!" She was startled a moment by the ogre. He looked— different.

"Alexandra, meet Yogi Ogre. I licked all the yogurt off of him. He cleans up pretty well, don't you think?"

"You realize, don't you, that yogurt is basically moldy milk?"

"It's wha . . .sputter, sputter, cough . . . Oh, no bother. My mother always said: What doesn't kill you, makes you stronger."

"You'd better hope that's true if you just licked every inch of an ogre. No offense, Yogi."

"None taken," said Yogi Ogre with an impish grin and one finger against his lips.

Yogi Ogre looked much less fearsome without slime dripping off his entire body. Now he looked like a big, comical creature with a dopey grin.

Alexandra continued: "Donkey Oatie, if you're done with your yogurt-fest, we need your help—both of you."

As King Daggerhammer reacted to Peter's verbal challenge, he drew his sword and ordered his men to back away. A clap of thunder rolled in the distance.

King Daggerhammer stared at Peter's glowing blade and waited for the boy to make the first move. Peter lunged forward for a quick thrust, but King Daggerhammer blocked it. "Why does your blade glow like that?" asked the king.

"Why doesn't yours? I thought all blades glowed in a fight." Peter knew this wasn't true, but if his blade intimidated his opponent, then that was a good thing. He wasn't about to explain what he didn't understand, anyway.

Someone in the crowd yelled: "Look! His sword is glowing!"

There were gasps among the crowd as Peter's blue blade cut through the increasing darkness caused by the storm and nightfall. The crowd seemed mesmerized by each swing of the glowing blade.

Then the two swordsmen clashed blades several times and Peter attempted a sidearm swing at King Daggerhammer. The king mostly blocked the blow, but Peter did rip the King's robe.

Peter thought Daggerhammer might be an easy opponent, with all those heavy royal robes and the excessive jewelry weighing him down, but the man's great strength and experience offset his fashion hindrances.

More thunder rolled in the distance as a storm drew nearer.

This time King Daggerhammer made a sudden move for Peter's weak spot, his undefended left side. Peter thought, *If I get out of this alive, I really need to get a shield, and maybe some armor.* Peter backhanded a defensive move and then countered with a swipe back at Daggerhammer's torso. Again his opponent blocked it.

Peter had some training with a sword, but more in the technical ability than in strategy. After all, fighting the dragon was different because the dragon didn't swing a sword back at you.

He decided to try some moves that were unconventional enough they might throw the king off balance.

King Daggerhammer attacked again and Peter blocked the blow, but rather than return to a defensive posture, Peter took a swipe at the king's knees. It worked. The king reacted slowly to this unexpected move and Peter drew blood.

The crowd of people had been watching with great interest and became increasingly involved in the sword fight. They began to gasp, cheer, and sneer as one opponent or the other seemed to have the upper hand.

The two swordsmen circled each other on the platform. Thunder clapped, much nearer. Then lightning brightened the sky. Peter and the king exchanged a series of blows and, after blocking a blow, Peter swung his body around in a full circle and came at the king with the full force of his blade.

The king partially blocked it, but Peter still got a good hit. It would have been much worse, of course, if the king wasn't wearing such thick robes, which were beginning to look quite shredded.

Peter was aware of fighting on the balcony above him, but he focused on the king's moves. The king was beginning to move unevenly.

Sir Wendell walked up to the gate to release the prisoners. Two of King Daggerhammer's soldiers blocked the way and drew their swords. Sir Wendell laughed. "Are you sure you want to do this, boys?" He stepped aside and the guards saw an ogre.

They stood their ground until the ogre walked up to them. The ogre let out a ferocious roar. The soldiers took off running but the ogre grabbed them. With one in each enormous hand, he held them down in front of Sir Wendell, who searched them until he found the keys.

Then the ogre let out another ferocious roar and dropped the soldiers, who scrambled to their feet and ran off.

Yogi Ogre had been detained in this cell earlier in the day. Now he was more than happy to have the honor of unlocking the crank box and turning the crank handle. The iron gate lifted to release the captives.

Donkey Oatie said, "Yogi Ogre, not only do you have good taste; you are bad to the bone!"

People flooded into the courtyard after being released from their nearby captivity. "Ach! What's that?" cried someone. A burst of lightning brightened the sky enough to show the outline of a dragon flying overhead. People began to scream, "A dragon! It's a dragon!" But their fear was overcome by fascination as they joined the others to watch the drama unfolding on stage, where a boy with a glowing sword dueled the invading king. They could see another swordfight happening on the balcony above.

Another clap of thunder rumbled through the sky. Immediately, lightning lit up the sky and darkened the hearts of those watching. Then it began to rain, an ominous sign to those who believed in such signs.

Sir Cumference and his men formed a perimeter and Sir Loin and his men began to confront enemy soldiers. Everything was going as planned. But they sky was growing dark and the ominous storm grew more threatening as severe winds buffeted an already battered people.

Nobody seemed to notice it over the sounds of the storm, but the seven giants, at the instruction of Alexandra, began destroying the machines of war outside the city wall. King Daggerhammer's army had cannons, catapults, battering rams, ladders, and other devices. The giants stepped on them, threw them, smashed them into each other, or crushed them like eggs.

"They won't be using these again," said Lofty.

Donkey Oatie trotted around the courtyard in the dark and rain, looking for his friends among the large crowd of people gathering. The crowd seemed to be watching something. Donkey Oatie looked where the crowd was looking and saw twin swordfights going on—one up on a balcony and another on the royal platform.

"Peter! Hey, that's Peter—the one with the glow-in-the-dark sword," said Donkey Oatie to all the people around him. "Peter is the rightful king of Mirabeau. He's the son of

King Cole." Donkey Oatie continued to wander through the crowd, explaining what people were watching.

When a flash of lightning brightened the sky, two dragons could be seen circling over the castle. Someone yelled: "Look! There are *two* dragons!" Screaming ensued. In the darkness above, two dragons circled overhead as if they were selecting a prey to pounce on.

Donkey Oatie wrinkled up his face. "I don't know where these dragons came from. I thought we killed the last remaining dragon in Dragon Hollow. Let me tell you about the time Peter and I faced the dragon."

Sebastian continued to fight Grimbald. The balcony created a confined area for them, which meant less room to evade and regroup, but it also meant keeping your opponent close at hand.

It became a high-contact swordfight for there was no room to circle around, staring at your opponent. In blow after blow, the two swordsmen met the challenges of their opponent. Both had incurred some minor flesh wounds. And both were growing tired.

As the darkness grew and the thunder and lightning grew closer together, Sebastian knew he needed to end this soon or he wouldn't last much longer. Then, in a lapse of concentration or an unexpected move by Grimbald, Sebastian found himself pinned down by Grimbald's left forearm. As Grimbald pushed him farther and farther over the balcony rail, Grimbald used his right hand to draw another dagger from his black cloak. He held the dagger high in the air, ready to strike.

Peter saw Sebastian pinned down on the balcony rail above him. "Sebastian!" Then he saw the dagger glisten in a flash of lightning. As the dagger hung in the air over Sebastian, Peter yelled, "Noooo!"

A fresh burst of adrenalin burst through Peter's veins and he fought King Daggerhammer with renewed vigor. He was ready to end this once and for all. He laid both hands on his heavy, adult-sized sword and chopped with it, trying to land a hard blow on King Daggerhammer for once.

For just a moment, he took his eyes off of the king to check on Sebastian. He couldn't see him in the dark and rain. "Sebastian!" That's when King Daggerhammer flipped Peter's glowing sword right out of his slippery, wet hands.

The sword did a summersault through the air and the crowd of people scattered to get out of the way. Peter's sword landed point first in a narrow strip of dirt between the cobblestones. His sword stood there in the courtyard like a barren tree. It reminded Peter of when he had first pulled it from the stone in the courtyard at The Magic Kingdom.

In the instant the blade landed in the courtyard, another crack of lightning with a simultaneous burst of thunder shook the ground with tremendous force, knocking people off their feet. The bright flash of lighting blinded everyone for a moment and then there was a collective gasp among the crowd.

The lightning had struck the sword. The ground all around it was scorched and smoldering. The blade glowed blue, even more intensely than before. And the hilt and handle had turned molten red.

Peter got to his feet and leapt off the platform. He took several steps toward his sword. He wasn't sure about the handle. He had never seen this. Yet something in him told him to take the sword, so he turned his body to align with the handle and wrapped his fingers around it.

The handle of his sword was hot, but not painful. As he pulled the blade out of the ground, he felt the hot handle conform to the shape of his hand. Then, the falling rain turned to steam as it hit the handle and cooled it.

The blade was still glowing from the lightning strike. Peter laid it across both hands and studied the blade. He could read the inscription!

He read one side, with text running almost the full length of the blade, and then he turned the blade over in his hands to read the other side. Then he dropped to his knees. The heavy rain washed away the tears running down his face.

Chapter 19
Armed and Dangerous

Peter rose to his feet and stood in the pouring rain. He looked at all the dead bodies around the courtyard. He saw the frightened or bewildered looks of soldiers and citizens standing in the rain watching him.

He held up his glowing sword and lifted it above his head until his arm was fully extended. He slowly turned his body in a circle to face the onlookers in every direction as he yelled:

"People of Mirabeau, rise up and fight. Take back what has been taken from you this day. Take back Mirabeau!"

A mighty battle cry arose among the crowd and people began to take action. Some citizens picked up the weapons of fallen soldiers and began to fight the enemies. Others ran toward the castle to round up the enemies.

Peter climbed the stairs two at a time to get to the top of the platform one more time. "You're done, Daggerhammer. Surrender or die!"

"Never!" shouted Daggerhammer as he thrust his sword at Peter.

This time Peter swung his blade—but it seemed lighter now for some reason—and it sliced the king in the neck. The king dropped to his knees. Peter thrust his sword in Daggerhammer's belly. The man coughed and sputtered and fell over dead.

Many in the crowd cheered that the invading king had been defeated. Then, the two dragons swooped down for a closer look and the crowd screamed and ran for cover.

Peter looked up at the dragons, but didn't have time to waste. He would deal with them later. He cleaned his sword and ran into the castle. He ran up two flights of stairs. His heart was pounding for fear of what he might find. He ran out to the balcony.

It took a moment to sort out what he could see in the darkness. There was a lifeless body. Then Peter stepped forward and saw Alexandra holding her brother, with his head resting on her lap. "Alex?" asked Peter, his voice wavering. "Is he . . ." Peter couldn't even say the word.

"Peter!" she said. "He'll be all right. He's wounded and exhausted. When I saw Sebastian being pushed over the balcony rail, I readied my bow and when Grimbald raised his arm with the dagger, I was able to get a clear shot—an arrow right in the heart."

"What a relief!" exclaimed Peter. He sank to his knees next to them. "You're amazing with that bow, Alex."

She looked away, a little embarrassed.

"Really. I mean it. That was an incredible shot, made with precision aim and timing—and you saved your brother's life."

"Thanks, Peter."

As Peter returned to the courtyard to see what needed to be done, he could hear Donkey Oatie. He was on the platform telling the people all about Peter and his heroic adventures. He told about destroying the dragon and the evil sorcerer.

"And now, he's helped save Mirabeau from two evil kings who would have been evil dictators and tyrants. You are so lucky to have someone like Peter for your next king. He is, you know. Peter is the son of King Cole and the rightful heir to the throne."

The two dragons circled lower and lower over the courtyard. People began to scream again. The dragons hovered over the courtyard, flying in place like dragonflies. "Peter! Are you okay?" asked one dragon.

Peter stepped forward for a closer look, wondering if what he was thinking could be true.

Some of the soldiers began shooting arrows at the dragons and someone fired a small canon into the air. Donkey Oatie said, "Hey! You don't want to be doing that! You don't want to make a dragon mad. He'll bite you in half. I've seen a dragon bite a mountain goat in half. I don't want to see that again. I'll be so scared, I'll wet my pants. Oh, wait, I'm not wearing any pants."

While Donkey Oatie chattered nervously, he wasn't the only one getting nervous. All of a sudden one of the dragons turned red hot and burst into flames in the night sky.

"Whoa!" said Donkey Oatie. "Hey, wait a minute. Are you related to that little flaming gecko?"

"I am Grudge."

"How'd a little Grudge turn into a great big Grudge all of a sudden? And could you write my name in the sky while you're all flamed up because I've always wanted my name in lights?"

"Grrrrrrr."

"I'll take that as a no," said Donkey Oatie, cowering away and hiding behind Peter.

Peter stepped forward on the platform. "Grudge? Hunch? What are you doing here—like this?"

The people were in awe as Peter conversed with the dragons, who had now landed in the courtyard and were talking eye to eye with Peter on the raised platform.

Hunch explained: "All the battle noise—the canons, sword fighting, and screams—made Grudge glow red hot and burst into flames. He was running around crazy-like and stuff was catching on fire so I chased him into the stream to cool him off. Boy, I had no idea he would expand like that in water. Then, when I saw he had become a dragon, I wanted to be one, too, so I ran into the stream and look what happened! Pretty fearsome, huh?"

"Wow, boys! I never dreamed you would, um, grow up so quickly."

Before they could reply, Hunch and Grudge looked around as if startled by something. They took off flying and began to circle overhead again. Grudge broke into flames again and did a nosedive toward the city gate.

Horns blew in the darkness, cutting through the rain like a knife. Sounds of riders on horseback entered the city. They wore armor. "Another army!" shouted a citizen.

"No, wait!" said Peter, who stepped forward.

King Arthur rode up to the platform. "We came as quickly as we could, but it looks like we are too late, Sir Peter."

Donkey Oatie said to the crowd: "Oh, and did I mention Peter is one of King Arthur's Knights of the Round Table?"

"Thank you for coming, King Arthur. We still need your help. We need help gathering up the soldiers of Cadence who invaded us today, and also the soldiers loyal to King Burger who betrayed his own people." Peter waved his arm around at the scene of the battle. "We also need help gathering up our wounded and dead."

"Of course, Sir Peter. We will do everything we can." Then King Arthur gave a few orders to his knights and turned back to Peter. "Shall we engage the dragons, Peter?"

"No, they're mine."

"That's a relief! I wouldn't want to engage one, much less two dragons!" King Arthur gave a few more orders to his knights before turning to Peter again.

"We will do what must be done tonight. But my men have traveled all day and your men have fought all day. We all need rest and we can put off much of it until tomorrow. I have ordered my men to see to security issues and to check among the dead for any who are still living and need medical help. The rest can wait until morning."

"Thank you. That will be fine."

Chapter 20
No Magic Cure for Pain

Peter slept later than he intended, but he rested well because he had been so exhausted. By the time he wandered out into the courtyard to survey the aftermath of the battle, the cleanup was already underway.

He sat down on some stairs watching people remove the bodies. There were dead soldiers from all three armies, but there were also many unarmed citizens who had been killed in the battle.

Peter's chest ached and he wanted to cry out of grief and anguish. He put his elbows on his knees and rested his head on his hands.

Then he felt a hand on his back and saw someone sit down next to him on the step. He looked up to see who was there. "Lucas!"

he exclaimed and he wiped the tears from his eyes. Then he threw his arms around the magician and said, "I didn't expect to see you here."

Lucas the Magician said, "I was in The Magic Kingdom when the rider delivered your dire message to King Arthur, so I traveled with the army and arrived last night. But last night, you had other things on your mind, so I waited until now to greet you."

There was a long silence. Peter wasn't sure what to say, but he knew he wanted to pour out his pain and frustration to his trusted advisor.

"I can't bear to see so much pain and suffering," said Peter, still gazing upon the carnage around him.

"Don't be afraid to see what you see," said Lucas the Magician, pausing to let that much sink in. "Closing your eyes to it means closing your heart to it."

"But it hurts to know I have caused so much pain to so many people," said Peter, finally admitting what he really felt.

"You have not caused this suffering, Peter." The magician paused and said, "Peter, look at me." Peter looked up with tear-stained cheeks. "You have not caused this suffering, Peter. Your actions stopped those who were inflicting the pain."

"The people of Mirabeau have lost

everything," said Peter.

"The people of Mirabeau have gained hope, Peter. You have given them great hope."

Chapter 21
Coronation

What a difference a week makes! thought Peter. He was peeking out the castle window at the massive crowd of people gathered in the courtyard. A week ago they were gathered to watch King Burger slay Peter, Sebastian, and Alexandra as traitors—and to make the people an easy target for King Daggerhammer's invasion.

With the help of King Arthur's men, the people had cleaned up the city and repaired some of the most significant damage. And the seven giants had gone beyond makeshift repairs and had thoroughly repaired the wall with stones and mortar. The giants accomplished in days what would have taken months for the people of Mirabeau.

Moreover, the people had a week to care for the wounded and mourn for the dead.

So many people of Mirabeau had lost friends and family members. But after a week filled with funerals, the people were ready to celebrate a new king.

That king was looking out the window with his stomach doing flip-flops.

"Peter? Is that you? Peter! You look . . . wow!" said Alexandra.

Peter was wearing a pair of brown satin breeches with matching stockings and new black, leather shoes. He wore a new white shirt with a royal blue tunic made of satin and a coat of scarlet satin, with poofy sleeves that had gussets of yellow. His sword and sheath were polished and hanging at his waist. At his feet sat a brand new shield and a royal staff adorned with jewels. His hair was freshly cut and his nails trimmed. He also wore a gold necklace that belonged to King Cole.

"What? Do I look okay? I look ridiculous, don't I? I told them I didn't want to wear all these fancy hoo-has."

"Peter, you look like a king!"

"And you look like a princess—no, a queen, Alex!"

He studied Alexandra as if he was seeing her for the first time. Her dress was a picture of elegant simplicity. He had never seen her in a floor-length dress, but this suited her and now he almost hoped he would never see her in anything else.

The dress was blue satin down to the floor with a short train that flowed behind her. The high neckline of the dress was adorned with a gold necklace. The dress was tight enough to display Alexandra's curves. Peter wondered when she had gotten curvy. She also had a light veil on her head, though it did not cover her face at the moment.

"What's the veil for?" asked Peter. "Are we getting married and I didn't know it? They told me this was a coronation ceremony, not a wedding."

Alexandra slapped him on the arm as she was accustomed to doing when they joked around.

"Hey! You just assaulted the king. I could have you . . ."

"You're not king yet. Technically."

"You can hit me anytime, Alex. How's Sebastian? He's going to make it, isn't he?"

"I'd have to be dead to miss this," said Sebastian who had been standing in the shadows watching the interaction between Peter and his sister, Alex. "You look very kingly, Peter."

"Sebastian! How are you feeling?" asked Peter.

"Fine. Just don't wrestle with me yet."

"Well, you look great," said Peter.

Sebastian wore black leather shoes, brown stockings and breeches with a white shirt and a sleeveless jacket made of reddish brown cloth. He, too, wore his sword at his waist. And he held a yellow felt hat with the brim turned up and fastened with a blue gem.

"I feel like a court jester," said Sebastian.

"No. That's my job," said Donkey Oatie as he bounded into the room.

"You're looking mighty fine, Donkey Oatie," said Alexandra. Donkey Oatie was bathed and brushed. Plus he had a string of flowers around his neck.

"Can someone help me take these flowers off so I can eat them? They smell delicious."

"After the ceremony. You may eat them after the ceremony," promised Peter.

"Is everyone ready? It's time," said Lucas the Magician.

"I'm nervous. I hope I don't throw up," admitted Peter.

"Oh, that will make a good first impression as king," said Donkey Oatie, rolling his eyes.

"You'll do fine, Peter," assured Lucas the Magician. "In fact, there's not much you have to do at all. Just let it all happen and enjoy the moment."

A trumpet fanfare echoed through the courtyard. Lucas led the three young heroes, followed by Donkey Oatie out the castle door. Peter extended his arm to Alexandra to formally escort her. Sebastian walked on the other side of Peter. Donkey

Oatie followed behind them.

The trumpeters continued to play a lively fanfare theme. Red and gold banners hung from their very long trumpets. Lucas led them on a red carpet the full length of the courtyard. All the knights of the kingdom lined the last section of red carpet on both sides.

"Smile, Peter," whispered Alexandra. "And you could wave at the crowd cheering for you." Peter smiled and raised his hand to acknowledge the crowd.

The crowd cheered even louder.

When they climbed the stairs to the platform, Sebastian, Alex, and Donkey Oatie stepped to one side of the throne and turned to face the crowd. Hunch and Grudge flew overhead and the crowd gasped. Then the two dragons landed on the ramparts of the castle, where they remained mounted as if overseeing the ceremony.

Peter dropped to one knee before the throne and continued to kneel while Lucas the Magician addressed the crowd.

"Citizens of Mirabeau and those gathered from other kingdoms, greetings. One week ago today, Mirabeau faced a turning point. King Burger, who made himself king, sold out Mirabeau to King Daggerhammer of Cadence. The battle was devastating, but it would have destroyed Mirabeau if it were not for the courage of Peter Cole, who rallied the troops loyal to the former King Cole and fought to defeat these usurpers and invaders."

"King Cole was my friend. To protect the heir to the throne from his enemies, he gave his son, Peter, to guardians who raised him as their own. After the first attack on Mirabeau several months ago, Peter and his friends, Sebastian, Alexandra, and Donkey Oatie went on a journey to destroy the dragon of Dragon Hollow. They defeated the dragon with the help of a special gecko named Peeve, who gave her life to ensure the ultimate defeat of the dragon. The two dragons you see here today are offspring of Peter's pet, Peeve."

"On their journey, Peter and his friends learned many things that will make them great leaders for Mirabeau. Their leadership, loyalty, and courage was demonstrated before all of you last week."

Lucas the Magician held up Peter's sword.

"Many of you saw Peter wield this sword against your enemies. The blade glows blue. I forged this sword and embedded it in a rock in The Magic Kingdom. Only the chosen one—the dragon slayer—would be able to remove it from the rock. Although many people tried, only Peter was able to remove this sword from the rock. The sword bears an inscription that can only be read when the blade glows blue. That inscription is significant."

> The sword of the Dragon King
> glows blue
> When wielded for purposes
> right and true.

"The sword itself—by its inscription and its glow in Peter's hands—confirms Peter as the Dragon King. You saw for yourselves how the sword turned blue in Peter's hand. He used it with a pure heart and honorable intentions. These qualities make him a trustworthy king. Do you here today appoint Peter Cole to be the King of Mirabeau?"

"We do! Aye! We do!" yelled the crowd and cheers erupted.

Lucas turned to Peter, who was still kneeling. With the sword he tapped Peter's left shoulder and then his right. "You carry the weight of Mirabeau on your shoulders. May the burden be light! Rise, King Peter!"

Applause and cheers erupted!

Peter stood, sheathed his sword, and announced, "I, Peter Cole, accept the responsibility of serving the people of Mirabeau as their king."

Peter and Lucas turned to face each other and Peter bent halfway from the waist. A crown bearer brought forward the crown on a red pillow with gold braid. Lucas took the crown and placed it on Peter's head.

Peter stood and the crowd erupted with cheers. Then they both turned to the crowd. Lucas the Magician announced: "People of Mirabeau, I present to you the Dragon King, Peter Cole!"

More cheers and applause filled the courtyard as King Peter took his seat on the royal throne—the throne of his father. One by one, each of the knights of the kingdom stepped forward and bowed before the throne to pledge his loyalty and life to the king.

Then Peter stood to address the crowd.

"People of Mirabeau, I don't know how to give fancy speeches, but I do have a few things to say. I will serve and protect you to the best of my ability until the day I die, but I need your help. I can't do it all and there is still much to be done to rebuild and restore Mirabeau. Only together can we make Mirabeau a place of peace and prosperity."

Cheers erupted in the crowd again.

"Second, I met dozens of orphans last week who have been homeless for several months since the first attack on Mirabeau. They need homes and apprenticeships. Please take these kids into your homes and hearts. They are the leaders of the future. Treat them well."

The crowd cheered their approval again.

"And, third, King Cole, my father, had dozens of fancy poodles as show dogs. I think these dogs would bring happiness to many more people if they were placed in homes. So, any home that takes in one or more orphans may come to the royal kennel and select a free poodle. May they bring great joy to the orphans and those who care for them."

Sebastian and Alexandra elbowed each other and stifled a giggle because Peter was terrified of poodles. He could fight a dragon, but he was scared of poodles. No wonder he wanted to get rid of the poodles right away.

At that moment, Grudge flew down from his perch on the ramparts. The crowd screamed and began to scatter. Grudge hovered low over the crowd and addressed Peter: "You call yourself the Dragon King but you killed my mother, Peeve."

Peter looked startled, but said, "I did not kill Peeve. Your mother gave her life to protect me from the evil dragon."

"Same difference. You were ultimately responsible for her death. And it is appalling that you claim to be the Dragon King now."

"Grudge? What are you doing? Can we talk about this later? Now is not an appropriate time."

Grudge was turning red hot and about to burst into flames. Peter was worried people would get hurt if Grudge flamed up.

"Roaaaarrr!" screamed Grudge as he climbed higher and burst into flames. People screamed. Grudge threatened Peter: "I want my mother! You killed my mother! But I'm not going to kill you. I'm going to make you suffer. You'll see." With that, Grudge flew away.

Peter looked up to see Hunch still sitting on the castle ramparts. Hunch shrugged his shoulders, not knowing what that was all about.

The crowd was murmuring and restless so Peter spoke again: "People of Mirabeau, I'm sorry such an incident disrupted the ceremony but, please, let us continue. And let me assure you that the conflict with the dragon will be resolved. I'm sure it's a misunderstanding."

Peter waved at Donkey Oatie to cue him. "Let's enjoy some music to lift our spirits," said King Peter.

Donkey Oatie stepped forward and said, "King Peter—Hee haw—it's funny to call you that. The seven giants who rebuilt our wall taught me this song. Because people seek the advice of kings and kings must be patient in giving advice, I dedicate this song to King Peter."

> There's a hole in the bucket,
> King Peter, King Peter,

There's a hole in the bucket,
King Peter, a hole.
Then mend it Donkey Oatie,
Donkey Oatie, Donkey Oatie,
Then mend it Donkey Oatie,
Donkey Oatie, then mend it.

With what shall I mend it,
King Peter, King Peter,
With what shall I mend it,
King Peter, with what?
With straw, Donkey Oatie,
Donkey Oatie, Donkey Oatie,
With straw, Donkey Oatie,
Donkey Oatie, with straw.

The straw is too long,
King Peter, King Peter,
The straw is too long,
King Peter, too long.
Then cut it, Donkey Oatie,
Donkey Oatie, Donkey Oatie,
Then cut it, Donkey Oatie,
Donkey Oatie, then cut it.

With what shall I cut it,
King Peter, King Peter?
With what shall I cut it,
King Peter, with what?
With a knife, Donkey Oatie,
Donkey Oatie, Donkey Oatie,
With a knife, Donkey Oatie,

Donkey Oatie, with a knife.

The knife is too dull,
King Peter, King Peter,
The knife is too dull,
King Peter, too dull.
Then sharpen it, Donkey Oatie,
Donkey Oatie, Donkey Oatie,
Then sharpen it, Donkey Oatie,
Donkey Oatie, then sharpen it.

On what shall I sharpen it,
King Peter, King Peter?
On what shall I sharpen it,
King Peter, on what?
On a stone, Donkey Oatie,
Donkey Oatie, Donkey Oatie,
On a stone, Donkey Oatie,
Donkey Oatie, a stone.

The stone is too dry,
King Peter, King Peter,
The stone is too dry,
King Peter, too dry.
Well wet it, Donkey Oatie,
Donkey Oatie, Donkey Oatie,
Well wet it, Donkey Oatie,
Donkey Oatie, well wet it.

With what shall I wet it,
King Peter, King Peter?
With what shall I wet it,

King Peter, with what?
Try water, Donkey Oatie,
Donkey Oatie, Donkey Oatie,
Try water, Donkey Oatie,
Donkey Oatie, try water.

In what shall I fetch it,
King Peter, King Peter?
In what shall I fetch it,
King Peter, in what?
In a bucket, Donkey Oatie,
Donkey Oatie, Donkey Oatie,
In a bucket, Donkey Oatie,
Donkey Oatie, in a bucket.

There's a hole in my bucket,
King Peter, King Peter,
There's a hole in my bucket,
King Peter, a hole.
Use your head, then!
Donkey Oatie, Donkey Oatie,
Donkey Oatie,
Use your head, then! Donkey Oatie,
Donkey Oatie, use your head!

The crowd laughed and sang along and erupted in applause when Donkey Oatie finished. King Peter rubbed Donkey Oatie's long ears and said, "Donkey Oatie has made it clear that he wants to be a royal minstrel, so for my first act as king, I hereby appoint Donkey Oatie as my official royal minstrel and court jester because he always knows how to brighten my day."

Donkey Oatie jumped up and down going "Hee haw. Hee haw. Hee haw." Finally, to get him off the stage, Peter took the chain of flowers off Donkey Oatie's neck and gave it to him. Donkey Oatie started chomping on the flowers and wandered off the stage to eat them. All of this was much to the delight of the onlookers.

"For my next act," said King Peter, "I hereby appoint and elevate Sebastian to the rank of knight." He motioned for Sebastian to come forward. "Kneel, Sebastian."

Peter touched his sword to each of Sebastian's shoulders and said, "For your friendship, loyalty, and courage, I name you Sir Sebastian, Knight of Mirabeau. Rise, Sir Sebastian."

When Sebastian looked up, Peter winked at him, but Sebastian's eyes were filled with tears because he wasn't expecting this honor.

King Peter raised his arms and said, "Thank you, people of Mirabeau." Then he took Alexandra's arm and with Sebastian on his other side, the three proceeded up the red carpet and back into the castle. Donkey Oatie trailed behind them with the string of flowers still dangling out of his mouth.

Chapter 22
Hidden Secrets

After the coronation, Peter was sitting on his bed, fiddling with his sword to pass the time. As he spun the sword in his hands, he thought he felt something move. He began to inspect the handle more closely.

The pommel at the base of the hilt was to provide a counterbalance and to keep one's hand from slipping. The weighted pommel was held on by a button. It was loose. Peter carefully unscrewed it and laid it on the bed.

Then he pulled off the pommel so he could see how it was assembled. But when he removed the pommel, it revealed a compartment in the hilt or handle. There was something inside his sword.

He poked his finger in the hole. He could feel the hidden object, but getting it out was tricky. He couldn't quite grab it. Then he held his sword vertical and tapped it to see if the contents would fall out. They moved. He alternately tapped the sword and poked with his fingers and the hidden contents began to emerge. Even when they were partway out, they seemed hung up on something.

Then he was able to lay the sword on his bed and pull out the contents. The first thing he could identify—and it was the item that kept hanging up as he tried to pull it all out—was a rather impressive ring.

Inside the ring was a small paper scroll, so he pulled it out of the ring. Inside the paper scroll was a small vial. When he took out the small vial, he noticed there was a tiny strip of paper wrapped around the vial and tied with a thread.

Despite the coronation, this was the most excitement he had felt all day. *What is all this stuff and why is it hidden in the hilt of my sword?* he wondered.

He spread the items out on his bed, looking at them with awe and curiosity. He picked up the ring. It had a blue stone—but he was a boy and didn't know what kind of gem it might be. *Perhaps Alexandra would know*, he thought. The ring was gold with dragons engraved in the band on each side of the stone. As he turned it over in his fingers he saw an inscription inside the band. *Not another inscription*, he thought. The inscription in the ring band read:

DRAGON RING

Peter thought it was a ring fit for a king but it was too big for him so he set it aside.

Then he picked up the scroll of paper and opened it with care. It read:

> The Dragon King will prove himself true,
> By restoring prosperity and peace anew.
>
> Dragons protected the cities of old.
> Of their valor, legends are told.
>
> But when the Dragon King will rise,
> The suffering people will cease their cries.
>
> To subdue a dragon, use the ring,
> And fulfill your purpose as Dragon King.
>
> Distribute dragons to cities once more,
> And warfare and bloodshed will stop, as before.

That was stunning. Peter held the paper

and leaned his head back against the wall. He recalled his book, *The Legend of Dragon Hollow*. It had talked about the prosperity of cities under the protection of dragons, but after the dragons were destroyed, that peace and prosperity was lost. The legend foretold a day when the dragons would return. Peter began to realize his role in this legend: to repopulate the dragons. But as the reality soaked in, so did the dilemma: He had a dragon out of control.

Peter turned his attention to the vial. It was about the size of his pinkie finger. He pulled off the thread and slipped off the tiny strip of paper. The vial contained a blue fluid of some sort. He unrolled the delicate strip of paper and read the tiny lettering:

> If injury creates a deathly need
> A drop of this tonic, healing will speed.

He thought: *I suppose that's a handy thing to keep in the hilt of my sword, in case I ever get a mortal wound in combat.*

Peter placed the papers and ring in the drawer of his bedside table. Then he slid the vial of healing tonic back in the hilt of his sword and reassembled it. He could hear the vial jingle around in the hilt, and he didn't want it to break, so he took it out and wrapped it in the handkerchief in his pocket. Then he pushed it all into the handle and reassembled it again.

It was still going to be several hours before the royal ball so Peter decided to sit down with his favorite book, *The Legend of Dragon Hollow*, and think about how this whole adventure began. He wanted to review what the book said about repopulating the dragons.

He reached in his backpack to get his book but he saw something out of place. He looked closely and found two new gecko eggs. He thought: *Repopulation is in progress but I'm not sure how I feel about having two more dragons when I can't even control the two I have.*

Chapter 23
Have a Ball

That evening, the castle had been decorated with special curtains, candles, and flowers. Table after table of food had been prepared by the kitchen staff. And people began to enter the ballroom, all dressed up in their finest clothes for the royal ball.

Peter wasn't too sure about this, but everyone told him the royal ball was tradition so he went along with it. He had never danced with a girl, and all he knew about dancing he had learned from his guardian-mother who taught him the proper stance and steps. Beyond that, he had no idea if he could dance well enough for a ball, especially with people closely watching their new king.

When Sebastian entered the ballroom, he

noticed Donkey Oatie over by the dessert and pastry tables. Sebastian approached him and said, "I'd ask you to dance with me, but that might be a little awkward."

Donkey Oatie went "Hee hee haw" and said, "Have you tried the oatmeal cookies? They're delicious! I had no idea adding sugar to oats and baking them would become such a tasty treat. From now on, I'll have Peter put these in the saddlebags for me when we go on a journey. Humans have so many creative ways to enjoy oats. I'm only beginning to appreciate the range of delicacies—from hot oatmeal to baked oatmeal cookies. Do you think anyone will care if I take home the leftover oatmeal cookies after the party?"

Sebastian smiled. "I'm not sure you'll have any leftovers at the rate you're going, but if there are, I'm sure King Peter would let his minstrel and court jester take a special privilege like that."

"That's good because when the giants introduced me to hot oatmeal, I thought that was taking oats to a whole new level. But now that I've had oatmeal cookies, I find that they've taken oats to a whole 'nother level!"

Sebastian wandered over to Peter and swiped a couple of fancy, filled pastries on the way. They stood by the wall eating them and watching guests enter the ballroom and mill around. Occasionally people would introduce themselves to King Peter and he would hide his pastry behind his back with one hand while cordially welcoming and thanking them.

Then he saw Alexandra enter the room. *What happened to that girl I used to climb trees with?* Peter wondered.

The music began.

Peter brushed the pastry crumbs off his hands and walked across the room to her. He took her hand and asked, "Miss Alexandra, may I have this dance?"

She giggled.

He led her out onto the dance floor and put a hand on her waist as they began to dance. Her dress was soft and silky. She looked up at him and said, "I've never danced with a king before."

Peter grinned and replied, "I've never danced at all before."

"Well, you're doing a fine job for someone who has never danced before."

"My guardian-mother taught me a little. But I've never danced with a girl, ahem, I mean, with a woman, until now."

Alexandra giggled again. He thought she had such an adorable giggle.

They danced in silence for a while.

Looking up at Peter, Alexandra asked, "King Peter, may I ask what is to become of me? I am, after all, an orphan. My best friend has become king and my brother has become a knight, but what about me? Am I to be placed in a family like the other orphans?"

"Alex, you have a family. Sebastian and I are your family. And you may have any position in my kingdom or my household you so desire. Name your preference. What do you want?"

"Queen?"

Peter laughed. "I should have known you'd be after the throne. Are you plotting against your king already?"

"Never."

"I know, Alex. You've always been a loyal friend, which brings me to my point."

He paused a moment and Alexandra said, "Speak, my king!"

"Very funny!" He made a funny face at her and continued, "Alex, if you have no strong preference to work in the kitchen or elsewhere, then I would like you to be one of my advisors. And it would mean we would still see each other all the time. But only if that's what you want."

"What I want? Of course I want to see you all the time, Peter. That's why I wanted to be queen."

"Really?"

"You are extending a great honor, Peter, but kings don't normally have women advisors, other than their queens."

"I'm not a normal king."

"You can say that again," she said, with a twinkle in her eyes while she softly slapped her palm against his chest.

He pulled her closer so she couldn't do that again.

As they continued to dance to the music, suddenly people in the ballroom started screaming and running for the exits.

King Peter looked up and saw Grudge's huge face peering in the doorway. He was perched on one of the balconies, with his head sticking through the doorway. Peter ran over to him, but Grudge withdrew his head and took off flying. Peter stepped out onto the balcony and looked up at the sky. He couldn't see Grudge anywhere.

People inside began screaming again and Peter stepped back into the ballroom. Grudge was on the opposite balcony. He stuck his head in the doorway and breathed out a huge blast of fire into the ballroom.

Before the smoke even cleared, Peter was trying to make his way through the room, but people were lying on the floor, crying or screaming. Peter's outer robe caught on fire so he took it off and threw it on the floor.

"I've got to put an end to this," Peter said through clenched teeth.

Grudge took off again. When he saw Peter step onto the balcony he said, "I told you! You killed my mother so I am going to make you suffer by hurting those you love. This is only the beginning, Dragon King!"

Sebastian grabbed Peter's arm. Tears ran down his smoke-blackened face. "Peter! It's Alex. She's badly burned. She's asking for you."

Chapter 24
Saving Alexandra

Peter ran to Alexandra, who was lying on the floor and a man was trying to move her. Peter put up his hand for the man to wait.

"Alex? I'm here for you. Don't worry, Alex, I'm going to get you the best doctors in the kingdom—and beyond, if I have to. Wait! I can do better than that."

Alexandra tried to open her eyes. "Peter," she said weakly.

Peter was unscrewing the end of his sword as he had done in his room earlier. He took the vial out of the hilt of his sword.

"Peter, if I don't make it . . ." she began.

"Alex, you're going to make it. I have a vial of healing tonic that will save your life and speed your recovery." He opened the vial and held it to her lips. *Just a drop*, he thought, as he forced himself not to give her the whole thing just to be sure.

Alexandra weakly licked her chapped lips and swallowed. Peter leaned forward and kissed her on the forehead and he remembered he had done the same thing after she had been injured by the dragon on Magic Mountain.

Then he sat back on the floor and gently lifted her head up on his lap as he waited to see if the healing tonic would work. He took her burned hand in his and gently held her with tears running down his face.

He felt dazed, as if everything was going in slow motion while he watched people tend to the other injured guests.

He also felt confused, as if everything was a dream or a distant memory. Had he really fought a battle to oust two kings a few days ago? Had he really been crowned king a few hours ago? Had he really danced with a beautiful young woman whose beauty had surprised him just a few minutes ago? Had he really grown up with, laughed with, cried with, and absolutely adored the fragile, wounded friend he held right now?

Alex moved a little. "It doesn't hurt anymore. The pain is gone," she said. Her voice was stronger.

"That's good to hear."

Peter waved one of the guards over. "Where are they taking the wounded?"

"They are gathering the wounded on the

mezzanine, where the royal physicians, Doctor Zeus and Doctor Who, are tending to them now, King Peter. Riders have gone out to summon every doctor in the kingdom with haste."

"Thank you," said Peter.

Someone yelled, "Look! The chandelier is burning!" People began to scream. The heavy ropes on the large iron ring of candles had caught fire in the dragon attack. The ropes had been slowly burning until they were now almost burned through and the fixture was tilting over the ballroom floor.

A number of people ran to get out of the way but other people ran to assist the wounded on the floor under the chandelier.

Peter said, "Sebastian, take Alex down to the mezzanine." He helped lift Alex into Sebastian's arms and watched his friend leave. Then Peter turned to help clear the area of all remaining injured.

A rope broke and the heavy iron ring jolted against the remaining ropes. People screamed again.

Peter assisted an older man with a limp. Once the man was clear of the scene, Peter went back to help a woman, but several men had placed her on a blanket so they could carry the blanket.

Just then, onlookers screamed again as another rope burned through and the chandelier jolted down again, but this time the jolt was enough to pop the remaining ropes and the whole thing jerked a couple times and fell to the floor with a thud that made the floor tremble. Peter and the others made it to safety just in time.

In the days and weeks that followed, Peter placed Alexandra in the room next to his and had doctors tend to her wounds daily in her private chambers.

Peter had many new responsibilities and spent long hours occupied with royal business in his new role as king, but as often as he could, he checked on Alexandra and was always relieved to find Sebastian with her while she recovered.

The doctors said Alexandra would fully recover her physical abilities, but her skin would be permanently scarred. The doctors marveled that she recovered so much more quickly than the others who had been burned and Peter knew he had the healing tonic to thank for that.

Alexandra's silky long hair had been damaged in the fire so her hair had been cut very, very short, but her scalp was undamaged so her hair would grow back in time. Peter had never seen her in short hair before and he thought it was kind of cute.

When she was well enough, they allowed Donkey Oatie in for a brief visit. "Miss Alexandra? Oh, you look wonderful. Why didn't you guys tell me she looked so good? I had no idea what to expect and no one tells me anything because I'm just a donkey. So I've been absolutely beside myself with worry. And let me tell you, it is no easy thing to come out of your body and sit beside yourself."

She giggled a little at his nervous chatter. "I'm glad to see you, too," she said.

"It's like my mother used to say: a friend loves at all times."

"Donkey Oatie, did your mother really say all the things you quote?" asked Alexandra.

"Well, no, but no one would listen to me if I said them. And it sounds more important, like bits of wisdom, if I say it came from my mother."

Peter, Sebastian, and Alexandra all laughed.

The end. But it's not really the end because there is always more to tell.

Blooper Reel and Outtakes

Chuck

> How much wood
> would a woodchuck chuck
> if a woodchuck
> could chuck wood?
> He'd chuck all the wood
> that a woodchuck could
> if a woodchuck
> could chuck wood.

Alexandra clapped in delight. Donkey Oatie said, "He's not that impressive. I can do it, too!"

> How much don
> would a donkey key
> if a donkey

could key don?
He'd key all the don
that a donkey could
if a donkey
could key don.

Chuck's eyes got big as he looked at his long-eared competition. "Want to see me chuck wood?" Without waiting for a reply, Chuck picked up a piece of firewood and chucked it at Donkey Oatie. It hit him in the shoulder.

"Ouch! He hit me! Did you see that? He hit me!" said Donkey Oatie.

"CUT! Let's save the animal violence for the dragon scenes, okay?" said the author.

Talent

King Burger paced back and forth a minute, looking at the faces in the room. "What's the donkey doing in here?"

"I came to apply for the position of minstrel." The kids in the room laughed. "I can sing, and dance, and tell dumb jokes, and juggle, and knit, and play cards, and play chess, and I can even rap and breakdance."

"CUT! Donkey Oatie, how many times do I have to tell you to stick with the script?" said the author in despair.

Don't Forget

"Now, let's see. I better not forget Peter's message before I get to Dirt Brown and the seven giants. What was that king's name?" said Donkey Oatie as he walked through the dark forest.

"Dag Kinghammer? No, that's not right."

"Kag Dingerhammer? No, that's not it."

"King Hammerdragger?"

"King Drag the hammer?"

"King Hammerjammer?"

"King Jibber Jabber? Hee hee haw! I amuse myself so often!"

"CUT! Donkey Oatie, let's just move on to arriving at the home of the giants. You don't always have to be such a ham!" said the author.

"Ham? No, that's the other king. I auditioned for him. King Ham Burger didn't appreciate my talents of singing and dancing. He had me escorted out. He was kind of rude."

The author shook her head and began typing again.

Audition

"I'm here to audition for the role of the second king. My name is Hot Dog."

"I can't have King Hot Dog fight against King Ham Burger. Whoever made the casting calls is fired," yelled the author.

Snoring

Donkey Oatie finished his oatmeal very quickly and while he was waiting for the giants to finish their meal, he fell asleep. He didn't mean to, but his stomach was full of warm food for the first time in his life and it made him all relaxed and sleepy.

Then he started snoring.

r-r-r-ronc shshshsh
r-r-r-ronc shshshsh
r-r-r-ronc shshshsh
r-r-r-ronc shshshsh

"CUT! Donkey Oatie! Stop snoring!" said the author.

"Oh, but I want to snore for this scene," said Donkey Oatie.

"That's not in the script," said the author.

"Gimme that script. I'll put it in," said Donkey Oatie.

Branded

Donkey Oatie looked in a mirror in his dressing room and got all worked up. "Look what he did to me! That flaming gecko put a gecko-shaped brand mark on my butt. I knew that hot little bugger would leave a mark. I'll never get another acting job! My career is over! Call my lawyer! Wait, I don't have a lawyer! Well, call animal control to come arrest that red-hot menace!"

The author had to intervene: "Donkey Oatie, settle down. Look! It brushes off. It was just a little ash left behind on your behind."

Cooties

While Alexandra was getting back up to her feet, the ogre grabbed her from behind. He picked her up and held her high in the air. The crowd gasped and some of the women screamed.

Sebastian's heart was beating hard. He walked up to the ogre and kicked him in the leg. "Hey, let her go! If you want a new toy, take me! Besides, girls have cooties!"

He knew if they survived this, he'd hear about that last statement, but he needed to get the ogre's attention.

The ogre dropped Alexandra and she went "uff" as she hit the ground. Then she stood up, put her hands on her hips, and began to lecture her brother.

"Girls have cooties? I'm about to be crushed and eaten by a giant ogre and all you can think of to yell is 'Girls have cooties!'?"

"Alex, I didn't mean it. I thought it might

make you distasteful to him."

"Distasteful?" She folded her arms across her chest.

"Oh, c'mon. You know what I mean. I was trying to save your life. And you're welcome, by the way!"

"CUT! Let's take that again from the top! Next time, let's save the family feud until later," said the author.

Sir Cumference

"Sir Cumference, have your men form a perimeter around the courtyard, including the occupying troops. We need to contain the battle and destroy any enemy who tries to retreat."

"I need to work on containing my own circumference because the perimeter of my waistline needs to be contained and it's every bit as much of a battle as fighting those enemies out there."

Stunned silence filled the room.

"CUT! Can we just stick to the script here, Sir Cumference? Let's try it again," said the author.

A Whopper

Alexandra came to the author in private and said, "Why do I have to get burned by the dragon? I think it would be much better if King Burger got flame broiled instead of me. If King Burger got flame broiled, that would be a real whopper!"

"Thanks for the suggestion, but I'll keep the script like it is," said the author.

Swedish Chef

After the dragon disrupted the royal ball, Oven the chef went to clear the banquet tables. He pulled up a chair and said, "My, oh my, look at all the food that needs to be put in the Oven!" Then he started eating and as far as anyone knows, he's still eating.

Read the Entire
Dragon Hollow Trilogy

The Legend of Dragon Hollow
The Secret of the Sword
The Rise of the Dragon King

Check out other fun stuff at

www.DragonHollowBooks.com

and check out the companion site for
young, aspiring writers

www.420BlackbirdPie.com

What's up?

Chuck the woodchuck

What's up?
Chuck the Woodchuck